The Town of the Cascades

Vol. 2

SALZWASSER
VERLAG

Michael Banim

The Town of the Cascades

Vol. 2

Reprint of the original, first published in 1864.

1st Edition 2022 | ISBN: 978-3-75259-532-1

Verlag (Publisher): Salzwasser Verlag GmbH, Zeilweg 44, 60439 Frankfurt, Deutschland
Vertretungsberechtigt (Authorized to represent): E. Roepke, Zeilweg 44, 60439 Frankfurt, Deutschland
Druck (Print): Books on Demand GmbH, In de Tarpen 42, 22848 Norderstedt, Deutschland

THE

TOWN OF THE CASCADES.

VOLUME II.

THE

TOWN OF THE CASCADES.

BY

MICHAEL BANIM

IN TWO VOLUMES.

VOL. II.

LONDON

1864.

CONTENTS.

A SEQUEL TO MY NARRATIVE.

CHAPTER III.

CHAPTER IV.

CHAPTER V.

THE

TOWN OF THE CASCADES.

CHAPTER XXVI.

DAY-DAWN.

None of the birds occupying the various habitats in the neighbourhood of the cascades had spent the night in the widow-woman's "lone room." Some of those birds had slept through the hours of darkness in the leafy grove; some in the close hedgerows; some in ivy-shaded clefts; some close-nestled in the moss beneath the gorse bushes; some in the dry grass, canopied by the fern. Not one of them had been in the "lone room," there to outrage the saints looking from the walls, or to scandalize the spruce Prodigal Son, or his most respectable father in bag-wig and flowered dressing-gown.

At the first upward glance of the ascending sun, when the very earliest tinge of dawn painted the eastern sky, every one of these birds, having imbibed no whisky-punch during the night, was up and stirring, while, as if in adoration, they poured forth their notes of welcome to the uprising source of light. On the topmost bough of the highest tree, as one conscious that the superiority of his music entitled him to the loftiest position, the speckled thrush sang his gladness-song, pausing between whiles, to bring to mind some excelling modulation he had been dreaming of. Less aspiringly perched, the blackbird sounded his flute-like, mellow pipe. From the bushes came the linnet's sweet warble, the goldfinch's merry carol, the impetuous notes of the chaffinch, the mellifluous warble of the robin, the piercing fife music of the wren. The black-cap in the reeds by the water-side prolonged his night-long ditty to aid the other feathered songsters of the morning. The swallow warbled as it took its primal air-bath. Even the single note of the swift, as it darted hither and thither, was modulated to music.

Not one bird dwelling in the neighbourhood of the cascades that did not rejoice at the return of day, and assist at early matins.

If there be any of my friends who have not heard the first morning hymn of the birds, I would advise him not to let another spring, or summer, or autumn dawn pass by, without going forth to listen to it. He will find that even unbidden, his heart will soar with the cheery song of the birds towards the throne on high whence gladness comes to the innocent, and to which the gushing melody he hears on every side ascends.

But—let him not go forth, as did Richard O'Meara, the conquering "king of the Gregory." Let him not go forth, as did Richard O'Meara, with unsteady gait, with rolling eyes, with hot, inflated breathing. Let him not dare, as Richard O'Meara dared, to scare the innocent and joyous birds from their adoration, by the discordant vociferation that bespoke not the heart's cheerfulness, but which was the canticle of insane, bravadoing recklessness.

As the birds in the neighbourhood of the cascades

hymned their matins to salute the approaching dawn, Richard O'Meara was wending towards his cottage shouting his canticle of recklessness.

His dog Teague, nearly recovered from the excitement produced by the liquor he had been compelled to swallow, preceded him. You would say that in the dog's knitted brows and troubled eyes, there was self-reproach and sadness. And as his master reeled behind him he paused constantly to look towards him—apprehensive for his safety.

The sun as yet had only limned with vermilion the light clouds hovering above his couch; elsewhere obscurity still prevailed.

Within a few yards of the Cottage of the Cascades, where some large trees stretched their branches across the road, there was yet the gloom of night. Here Teague scowled into the darkness, and growled threateningly. As if in answer to his challenge, a female figure, enveloped from head to foot in a dark-coloured mantle, emerged from the shade, and stood in the centre of the way along which Richard O'Meara came.

Teague recognized the intruder: he had modulated his growl from a notice of attack to a murmur of disapprobation, and took his place close by the muffled figure, muttering his dissatisfaction.

Richard O'Meara reeled along, unconscious of any obstruction to his progress, until he came in contact with the person standing silently to confront him.

"Hullabulloo!—hullabulloo!" he exclaimed as he recoiled; "who is it—that stands—here—to—impede—the royal—progress—of—the all-conquering king of the Gregory?—Eh?—who is it?—Answer, or I will—send you to the bastinado—and from the bastinado to the bowstring. Know—that I am no longer—a fiddle—I am "the king of the Gregory"—before whose prowess—all opponents—were forced to bite—the dust."

He changed his manner suddenly when a confused idea struck him that it was a female who stood so erect before him. He shook his head with owlish gravity, becoming in his own esteem exceedingly wise.

"Ellen, Ellen,"—he expostulated, "you are foolish, very foolish. Ri—di—cu—lous it is of you, Ellen, to be out in the—night—air—star-gazing. I know—you love me, Ellen,—and by my royal word, I love you in return. But—I will not—permit this. Ellen, my beloved wife that—you are,—I will use a fond husband's authority to prevent it. You have been drooping and sickly of late,—and unreasonable hours—spent out in the cold of the night—I must—interdict. I must and I will, Ellen, my dear wife,—I must and I will—interdict it——"

"May my heavy hatred, and my bitter curse, follow your Ellen every turn she takes from her rising to her lying down!" broke in the person Richard O'Meara addressed as his wife. And as she spoke, she cast the hood of her mantle back upon her shoulders.

"Ha, ha, ha!—This is Nora Spruhan I am lecturing, and not my wife Ellen,—ha, ha, ha!" It was the mockery of a laugh that Richard O'Meara laughed.

"Ay, Nora Spruhan I am, not your wife

Ellen. Nora Spruhan I am, and I am come, in the darkness,—in the darkness to be followed by no day-dawn for me,—to let loose the scalding of my heart, so long burning inside of it."

"Ha, ha, ha!—Nora, my girl,—'tis a myth, that scalding of the heart. Ha, ha, ha! no such ailment in reality."

And he sang out lustily, flourishing his hand above his head, while he sang:

> "This world, they say, is a world of woe,
> The same I do deny;
> Can sorrow from the goblet flow?
> Or pain from beauty's eye?"

"No—not at all—not at all—ha, ha, ha! had you been with us, to-night, Nora—upon my life and soul, you'd say—that sorrow—was—ha, ha, ha! —a goblin,—a phantasmagoria—without substance, —the semblance—the semblance only, of a monster, —who must flee as the devil flees from holy-water, the instant you dash a tumbler of hot, stout whisky-punch into his eyes,—ha, ha, ha, ha, ha!—ha, ha, ha, ha!"

And,—listen to me, Nora—. I'll tell you what —happens then—ha, ha, ha!—Im-me-diate-ly that you have well scalded the leaden eyes of sorrow— with the hot whisky-punch, mind it must be hot —hot—whisky-punch, don't forget that; the hot whisky-punch is far beyond wine for the exorcism. The moment, that you have well-scalded sorrow's leaden eyes, and that he makes his exit— howling—ha, ha, ha!—in comes a merry imp, all fun and frolic. Let me see;—upon my faith, I believe 'tis the same sprite makes his entry anew,— the gloomy black pall that had covered him flung away. He is now a—a Jack-pudding of a fellow,— I see him before my eyes at this moment, ha, ha, ha! A motley jacket and hose he has on,—flesh-coloured pantaloons, and great rosettes in his pumps, a tall, steeple-shaped hat on his nob, and a row of bells jingling about his jowl. Ha, ha, ha! And he dances, and capers, and sings;—he is a frisky, fantastic rascal, that he is. And he flourishes his bladder on the end of his pole,—and he bangs— right and left as he curvets about. And every one he bangs shouts as loud as he can shout,—and there is glorious merriment. Hurra, hurra! ha, ha, ha!—

"He that goes to bed, and goes to bed sober,
Falls as the leaves do,
Falls as the leaves do,
Falls as the leaves do,—
And dies in October.

"But he that goes to bed, and goes to bed mellow,
Lives as he ought to do,
Lives as he ought to do,
Lives as he ought to do,
And dies a good fellow.

Hurra!—hurra!—hurra!"

"'Tis the pity I could have for you, Dick O'Meara," interrupted Nora, vehemently and scoffingly. "'Tis the pity I could have for you, Dick O'Meara, if it wasn't that in the heart you have hardened, as hard as iron, there isn't any pity for any one."

"Blood, blood, Nora, girl,—don't be wicked. I'll—I'll—let me see—. Ay,—I'll solder up my ears, if you rattle your tongue at me. 'Pon my life and soul I will, ha, ha, ha!—solder up my ears to a certainty. I won't listen,—not I—not I—no, not I—"

"As sure as the sky is above our heads—you must and you will listen to me, Dick O'Meara. I could reckon years since I spoke out my mind in words. Often and often, while the years passed, did my teeth draw the blood from my tongue to keep the burning words unsaid. Listen to me now,—you must."

"'I think,' quoth Thomas, 'women's tongues of—ay of aspen leaves are made,'—ha, ha, ha! They rustle when—there isn't wind to bear up a midge;—upon my life, yes. Oh Lord!—oh Lord!—how they do whirl in the breeze, ha ha, ha!—Bring a steam-engine to a halt with your left hand—you might;—stop a woman's tongue with both hands, you couldn't. I defy you—ha, ha, ha!—But Nora,—mind me now,—don't knock the pins from under the merry-Andrew I told you of. Mind that, ha, ha, ha!—"

"It was this day eight years I met you first, Dick O'Meara."

"Agreed, nem. con., the premises granted."

"In my cousin Pat Malone's tent it was, where you came in and sat down beside of me."

"No wonder I should sit beside you; your black eyes were magnets. Your eyes were—

'As black as Kilkenny's own coals,
And through my poor bosom they burnt two big holes—'

ha, ha, ha! They did so—ha, ha!—"

"At the races of the sand hills, near to the say it was."

"Agreed again. By the life, I was flush in money that day. I won on O'Brien's 'Morgan Rattler.'"

"I was a very young crature then, an' I didn't think there was deception in the world. From that time out, I met you every day. You said you were filled with the burning love for me, and I gave credit to your words. But they were lies, black lies you spoke to me, Dick O'Meara!"

"My soul, but you are becoming furious, Nora. Down, Teague, down, dog! Take care,—he does not like your temper, Nora."

Teague's growl had become an ominous bark.

"Ay, hulloo him at me if you want to stop my words; but I tell you that if his teeth were fastened in my throat I would say what I came here to say. Neither you nor your dog can close my lips. The door of my father's house was shut against me, the neighbours jeered me, and turned their backs on me, and on my shame. I had no roof to cover my head—"

The levity of inebriety passed away from Richard O'Meara, and was replaced by a stupid sullenness. He was awed, too, by the girl's impetuous accusations.

"Nora,— Nora—" he expostulated angrily.

"Ay, ay!—I have the undherstanding of what you would say to me. You gave me shelter in your house, you would say;—and so you did. I came, and was your kitchen servant. Well content was I to be your servant. But—, Dick O'Meara!—without a warning given to me, you brought one home to be the mistress while I was the worker in the kitchen;—the worker for you and her!—"

"Nora!—" A second attempt at angry expostulation.

"Whisht, man,—whisht again!—I know what your words would tell. You said to me, you would give me a home in another place,—in another land where none would know me. And I made answer to you,—'No—No!'—And that *No* was the same as if my book-oath was given. I didn't tell *why* I said that No to you. I'll tell you now. I came here to tell it."

Nora brushed her brow and cheek with the lower extremity of her mantle, while she paused for an instant to take a lengthened respiration.

"You brought a wife across your threshold. *I* skulked in the hall to fasten my eyes on her. If I saw one coming in to be the mistress unsightly to look at;—if I saw that you were her husband for lucre sake;—what great matter would it be? But no,—no,—no!—To my grief I saw a young crature, comely and fresh, and blooming as an early morning in May. I knew, at the very first look, that the love promised to Nora Spruhan was taken from Nora and given to this stranger. From the moment my eyes lighted on her, the heart withinside of my body was changed from flesh and blood to hard iron. It couldn't have the love in it longer for any one;—and the rank hatred of the iron heart was upon you and your fresh, comely wife.

"But I wouldn't go. No. I said to myself that I wouldn't stir from the same house ye lived in;—that I'd stop in it to have my revenge on both in some way or in some how. The iron heart of the cast-off Nora said to her, 'Fasten your fingers in her white neck, and tighten them round it, and then let her fall a breathless corpse.' The iron heart said this to the cast-off Nora. And she would have obeyed it if she could!—Ay—and she'd face the judge upon the bench without fear or shame, if the one that took the love from Nora lay dead at her feet."

"Nora," said Richard O'Meara, "you are, by God——"

"Whisht, man!—Call no names; you have no

right to call me out of my name. What I am, *you* made me.

"But the fresh young wife was well guarded from me. You guarded her; Michael Hanrahan guarded her; others guarded her; and I did her no harm. No thanks to me for that.

"Dick O'Meara, open your ears to my words!—Whisperings and colloguings I heard, and the hearing of my own ears, and the sight of my own eyes gave me to know,—that the curse coming from the iron heart of Nora Spruhan was falling;—on you that changed that heart to iron, and on the one that took the love from Nora, to make prize of it herself. Day and night, Dick O'Meara, my watch was upon you. 'No need for you, Nora Spruhan,' I said down in my kitchen, 'to tighten your hands round the white throat of the one that came here, so fresh and blooming, and happy. No need for you to run the venture, and to do the sin. Dick O'Meara his own self will give food to the craving of your hatred.'

"Dick O'Meara, you are this night levelled with

Thomas Monahan that lies helpless drunk in the streets of the town, for the passers-by to toss from their road. And the young, blooming, comely wife, will soon be in her early grave. And she will be driven there by you, not by the iron-hearted Nora!

"I came out to meet you face to face, and to tell you this. That the wrong done to Nora Spruhan will be avenged by the one that wronged her."

Nora turned suddenly, and disappeared among the trees. Richard O'Meara wavered for a while where he stood. The dawn, looking down on his face, saw an expression of stupid horror there. He reeled, and fell heavily on the road.

Michael Hanrahan had been a witness of the scene just described. He came from his concealment, and with his aid and the aid of Teague, who seized the overpowered drunkard by the collar, and held him in a sitting posture, until Michael, with great exertion, raised him to his feet,—Richard O'Meara gained his cottage.

CHAPTER XXVII.

"OUR ANGEL'S" SORROWS.

It is not necessary for my purpose to signify the length of time that had gone by between the closing of the last Chapter and the commencement of this. I have before notified my intention of recording the most prominent occurrences only, that marked the progress of Richard O'Meara into the mire wherein irreclaimable drunkards sink;—whence they scarcely ever emerge.

It was a genial day in April. Shadow playfully veiling sunshine, and sportive sunshine emerging laughingly to chase away the shadow, the "sun-showers" of April falling, as the shadow flitted from the sun-burst. Gently the drops came down,—barely sufficient to moisten the wings of the breeze that gambolled along the water above the bridge of the cascades, soared over the waterfalls, skimmed under the arches, and fluttered through the tender foliage rising above the river where it flowed placidly onward.

On this particular day, no matter after what lapse of time, Michael Hanrahan rested both his elbows on the parapet of the bridge, frequently referred to, and gazed meditatively into the water beneath. Shoals of ephemera, born of the sunbeam of spring, sailed along the rippling surface of the river before it plunged downwards, and the trout, all on the alert, ascended incessantly to snatch the manna provided so abundantly for them. But although, through the transparent medium, the brisk and graceful motions of the speckled denizens therein could be well noted, Michael Hanrahan evinced no interest. I doubt that his eye took cognizance of them at all. His gaze was intent and earnest, no doubt, but his brain was so engaged with inward cogitations that outward speculation scarcely painted a picture thereon.

He was roused from his reverie by a startling

bang against the flag-stone immediately at his right elbow. The sound was produced by the blackthorn cudgel of the Half-pay, and the thwack was purposely given to attract Michael's attention.

"Ho!—Curnel. Good morrow and good luck."

"Maw!—Maw!" saluted the Half-pay. "Well—all?" he inquired; and he pushed his arm straight from him, and pointed the blackthorn in the direction of Richard O'Meara's cottage.

"Ullaloo!—well, indeed!—anything at all you like *but* well, Curnel. The meeaw and the misery is on us,—the heavens be our help this day!—The grief and the sorrow is under our roof;—the grief and the sorrow is in the one home with us,—and won't quit us, I'm afeard."

"How?—Why?—"

"As to the how and the why, Curnel,—there is no witchcraft wanting to find that out."

"How?—Why?—" the Half-pay repeated;—and he punched down his cudgel and his composite leg simultaneously, thereby denoting eagerness and excitement.

"What brought Sorrow to come and put up his quarters with us, Curnel, was this ;—"

And Michael doubled the fingers of his right hand against his palm, placed the resemblance of a tumbler so formed, in contact with his lips, threw back his head, and looked towards the sky.

"That is what brought it all on us, Curnel, my deary!"

Michael's appellation of "my deary" to the Half-pay had no kindness in it. The tone of voice changes the meaning of words materially, and the Half-pay understood that he was not Michael Hanrahan's "deary" at all, although so called by him. My schoolmaster, when I was a lad, used to call the boy he intended to flog his "deary."

"How?"

The Half-pay made a tumbler of his hand as Michael Hanrahan had done, placed his fist to his mouth, threw back his head as Michael had done, and looked to the sky as Michael had done. The language of signals suited him best, and Michael was not ignorant of this.

"How?" the Half-pay again asked, quaffing a second time from his figurative goblet, and looking very resolutely at Michael, when he had finished his aërial draught.

"I'll tell you that same, Curnel. Our poor Masther Dick is as grand a looking boy as you'd find footing the sod anywhere at all; and he has a warm and a loving heart inside of him as you'd find at the end of a year's journey, thravel as fast as you could. But *go vic och a dhiea urth*, he's a soft ownshuch of a crature that's easily led, and he followed the bad example that was set before him. He took on to the liquor, my heavy hatred be upon it for liquor! And the dhrink brought wickedness, and ill-temper, and sourness. And with the sourness and ill-temper, sorrow walked over our threshold. Now you have it. May the Lord forgive them that brought our grief upon us by their sinful example."

"Who?" the Half-pay vociferated, with apparent ferocity.

"I won't take long to tell you who they were, Curnel. One of them is that shivering, shaking Ned Culkin the gauger; another of them is creeping, skulkin Tom O'Loughlin;—and another of them is your own sweet self, Curnel, my deary."

As Michael again addressed the Half-pay as his "deary," with a modulation of voice little befitting the term of endearment, he turned full round, rested his back against the parapet of the bridge, and looked directly into the face of the person he spoke to. There was deep sadness in his big, grey eyes, and his fleshy lips drooped as if he were about to weep.

The Half-pay's brows were drawn tightly together until they met above his nose. From the point of contact, three deep furrows radiated, very seldom seen there;—and while his breathing came in laboured puffs, he looked as if he would perforate Michael's brain through his eyes. Michael's sad look did not quail before "the Curnel's" scowl.

"I came here, Curnel," he said, speaking slowly and affectingly, "on the chance of meeting with you on the owld spot, and I knew the hour to come. And I came to tell you our forlorn state, and to ask of you for the Lord's sake to give us your helping hand to push the sorrow back again over our threshold."

The Half-pay was visibly affected by Michael's speech and manner. Instead of delivering himself verbally, however, of his emotion, he flourished his cudgel over his head, meaning thereby that he was deeply interested. He stumped a few paces towards the descent of the bridge, and back,—the interpretation of which Michael rightly took to be, "Go on!"

Accordingly, with the Half-pay again frowning intently into his very eyes, Michael continued:

"If ever there was an angel sent—to fix itself in a cottage, that angel was sent to live under the same roof with us. And a blessing came with our angel when she walked up the garden-walk, and undher the porch, and into the hall. And the sunshine was round us and about us;—inside of the cottage, and outside of the cottage, the winter's day as well as the summer's day. The sunshine came with our angel, and it shined on us everywhere!"

During the whole of this poetical eulogium, the Half-pay's beaver was raised as high as his arm could elevate it, and his head bent.

"Our angel had a comrade she might be proud of; sightly to the eye, loving, and tender, and careful of her;—one that was able and willing to keep the thorns or briers or rough stones from her path, and to make it smooth like the soft grassy sod undher her feet. And the sunshine that the angel brought fell straight on him;—oh!—there wasn't one happier, gayer fellow living on Ireland's ground!—"

The Half-pay twirled his cudgel above his head, expressive of enthusiastic assent to Michael's fluent oration.

"We were prosperous, as well as happy, so we were. But the enemy of God and man had envy of us, like the envy he had of the poor couple in Paradise. And he came in among us, and he tempted the comrade of our angel with the liquor.

And he, the poor fool of a man, drank the liquor at the devil's prompting. At the first going-off he didn't take a heavy share, but by day and by night the enemy tempted him, and more, and more, and more he dhrank,—more and more every day. And then he'd wrangle with us, and he'd tell foolish lies that his own bungling tongue would prove to be lies, when he spoke them. And he'd say to our faces that we belied him;—that he didn't dhrink at all. We were asthray for a while to know where he got the liquor, but I found it out."

Michael paused to take breath. There was no twirl of the black stick this time, there was a consciousness in the Half-pay's unusually unsteady eye, that told he placed some of Michael's expositions to his own account.

"Curnel,—the enemy of God and man spewed a spawn of his on our flure, and that spawn he formed into the shape of a woman. By all accounts 'tis an owld thrick of his to turn God's best handy-work into tools for his thrade. A good young woman like our Mary is beyond the beyonds;—a bad young woman is the —— I'll say no more about what she is; 'tis the safest way!

"Well, Curnel, this spawn in the shape of a young woman gives help to her masther, the enemy of God and man. And when our poor misbeguided fool hides himself and takes the liquor, without any-one to see him, 'tis the spawn of a young woman brings it to him. I'm not without knowing why it is that she helps the enemy to destroy us;—I heard that from her own words. Often and often I did my best to banish her, but she won't depart from us. May the Lord forgive her—she is wicked!

"Curnel, Curnel, the dark, heavy clouds are over us and about us. Curnel, our sunshine is gone, and we are in darkness. Och!—Och!—Och! my grief it is that I have to say so!"

I have before had occasion to remark that Michael Hanrahan was not a stern, manly fellow in his deportment. At this portion of his narrative, his voice became tremulous, he entwined his fingers together, held both hands, so interlaced, before his chest, and rocked himself to and fro, as a woman in grief would do. The Half-pay drew in his breath with a cringe, and his troubled look winced before that of Michael.

"I have more to tell you," Michael continued, "and the worst of my story is to come yet. Our poor victim of a man dhrank, and dhrank, and dhrank of the liquor the tempter gave him. And by the means of it, often, and often, and often, it came about that he wasn't the light-hearted, laughing, loving, poor fellow that the Lord had made him to be. And the enemy put wickedness and sin into him with the liquor, and he was hard-hearted and cruel even to our angel—to the angel that he loved his own self beyond the life in his body. And he was a bugaboo to his childre. And he was all as one as a raging madman with his angel. And she shivered and shook before him. And she came to be like the flower the hail-storm falls on: she drooped her head, and she withered,—drooped and withered like the poor broken flower!"

Here Michael unlaced his fingers, and struck his hands together. The Half-pay banged his cudgel against the parapet of the bridge with the whole force of his arm. He shook his head impatiently, and dashed his hand across his eyes; but he did not succeed altogether in brushing away the tears that still moistened them as he resumed his gaze on Michael.

"The bitterest of all, I have now to say, Curnel."

Michael had passed his finger through a loop of the Half-pay's braided frock. He drew his listener towards him by this link. It was a very significant action; the Half-pay understood it to mean:—

"Let not one word of what I am now saying be lost on you."

"I am going to tell you what happened the very last night of all, Curnel. The little child that God sent us of late, is pining and decaying, the same way that our angel, its mother, is pining and decaying. Our angel had the wheeny, sickly, little child lying across her lap—and she was crying, and sobbing, and lamenting over it. Indeed, indeed, 'tis a hard heart that wouldn't grieve to hear her, and to see her. The poor Mary was sitting close by our angel, and she was shedding down tear for tear with the mother on the pale, gasping little child. Our poor deluded victim came in, and he reeled here, and he reeled there. At his bidding Mary left the room. I was outside, and she came close to me, and the door was banged against us. I could hear Mary's heart beating, and I am positive she could hear mine,—the both of us were in such fear. We heard an argument inside. The dhrunken man cried out for liquor, I could undherstand that. The poor angel had no liquor to give him, and then he called her names, and made a charge on her that she wanted to stint him in his own house, and that she must not attempt it. For the first time,—for the very first time since our angel stepped over our threshold, she spoke out to her husband from her bleeding heart—no wonder—no wonder, Curnel! But, Curnel!—I heard a blow given—och!—a heavy blow;—and I heard a long, loud cry, that went through me as if a sharp sword was sent into my breast—"

The Half-pay bounced, as if the same sharp sword had suddenly entered his body.

"I say it to you, that I heard the heavy blow, and the long, loud cry. I pushed the door wide open. Before I could take two steps another blow was given, and the third blow was given—given. Ay, the heavy hand of the sthrong man sthruck our angel the three blows. She fell down on the floor, and the puny, sickly little child, that she and Mary had been crying over, rolled away from her and lay helpless, wheening, and whimpering—'twas a sad sight to look on, Curnel——"

Michael burst into tears, and large, answering drops fell from the Half-pay's eyes, and ran along his cheeks—probably the first he had shed since childhood.

There was a pause. The Half-pay thrust the balls of his thumbs into the sockets of his eyes, and rubbed hard with them. He clenched his hand, and thrust it with the full force of his arm directly towards Michael Hanrahan's face.

"Struck her?"—he abruptly asked.

"Sthruck our angel!"

And Michael pushed his fist within an inch of the querist's mouth—thus replying by word and action.

The questioner hastened at his briskest pace down the descent of the bridge. He wheeled round, hurried back again, confronted the narrator of the outrage committed on the "angel," repeated the thrust forward of his fist, and barked out a second time—

"Struck her?"

"Sthruck our angel!" Michael Hanrahan again replied, again suiting the action to the word.

The Half-pay started off again, returned again, repeated his query in the same manner as before, receiving the same verbal and pugilistic reply.

The Half-pay fixed himself firmly, confronting Michael.

"Damn him!—damn him!—damn him!"

Three several times did he snap his jaws asunder

to utter his thrice repeated malediction. An unprecedented occurrence, be it known.

"This way I fastened in him—"

Michael seized both the arms of the Half-pay, and held his gripe as tightly as he could clench his fingers.

"Och hone, och hone! little chance had I to hold him."

And Michael's relaxing grasp allowed his hands to fall helplessly.

"He flung me down to his feet the same as if I wasn't bigger or sthronger than a chicken, and he kicked me with all his force. I'm wounded here, and here, and here," Michael touched his head in three places. "But I put my two arms round his legs, and I fastened my hands together. Little I cared about myself, but the dread was on me for our angel. If ever there was a raging madman, he was one. Never will I forget the staring and rolling of his eyes; never will I forget the foaming from his mouth as I looked up at him. Never to my dying day will his wicked oaths and threatenings lave my mind. Never—"

"Our—angel?" questioned the Half-pay, raising his beaver.

"While I was leaning over the bridge waiting for you, Curnel, I made up my mind on it, that 'twas the Lord, and the Lord only that put it into our angel's mind to act the way she did."

"How?"

"She recovered herself from the floor where she was lying, you'd think, dying,—like as if 'twas a miracle was worked on her. She snapped away the little, puny child from the arms of the shivering Mary; Mary, the crature, had picked it up. She made a run over; she raised up both the arms of its father; she put the wheeny child lying on them, and she pressed it against his breast. The poor thing whined a little whine; the madman looked down at it, and he wasn't a madman any longer. Ah! 'twas God himself that inspired our angel to bring the sickly little child, and lay it against his breast."

That the occurrence did take place, as described

by my friend Michael, is certain. That an almost instantaneous quietude—a supernatural calm, as it appeared to him—replaced the fell rage that had possessed Richard O'Meara is equally certain.

I should say that the wife understood, without any process of consecutive reasoning, that her maniac husband was to be subdued through his affections,—if subdued at all. And that her prompt and energetic proceeding was one of those impulses of woman's instinct which reach the mark, while man's more obtuse nature pauses. I should also say that she understood, still without reasoning (or if reasoning, only by a process like that of the despatch along the electric wire), that the helpless, pining baby placed, as Michael said, "against his breast," would appeal to Richard O'Meara's true nature, temporarily lost in the whirl of drunkenness.

And this explanation by no means interferes with Michael Hanrahan's doctrine of divine and special inspiration.

"Take your hands away, Michael," Richard

O'Meara said, bending down, and speaking in a whisper.

"Take your hands away, Michael; I will harm no one."

Michael believed the words whispered to him. He relaxed his grasp, and stood up. He was unsteady on his limbs, from the effects of the bruises he had received.

"Our angel," as in his new nomenclature Michael had dubbed his young mistress, was now kneeling, her hands joined, her terrified look riveted on her husband.

For a moment or two Richard O'Meara drooped his head over his passive, whining burthen. The scene so pathetically described by Michael had taken place in a bedroom. Richard O'Meara walked unsteadily to the bed. He laid the little child gently and cautiously on the coverlid; he looked apprehensively round for an instant, and then he went softly out of the apartment.

Ellen O'Meara rose from her knees. She tottered towards the bed where her infant lay, her shattered and overstrained nerves suddenly relaxed, and she fainted.

* * * *

Richard O'Meara, bareheaded as he was, passed out of his cottage, and into his garden. It was a very bright night, for the moon was at full. The "night-walker" did not take his way along the gravelled paths of his garden. Forward he went, trampling on the flowers, his progress figurative of his mental state, one would say. The zigzag print of his feet in the well-tended flower beds marked the directness of his course. He broke through the boundary hedge at the end of his garden; he scaled the boundary wall into the road. And over hedge and wall at the opposite side he made his way.

"Masther Dick, Masther Dick!"

Although his name was called in a whisper, the whisper fell as distinctly on his ear as if it had been a loud shout. He paused and turned round.

In the road he had just crossed, Nora Spruhan was standing, her face and figure fully recognizable in the white moonlight.

"I give you a caution," Richard O'Meara said, in a deep ominous tone of voice—"I give you a caution, to keep wide from the reach of my arm this night. If you follow one step farther, I will seize on you; I will take you, and fling you into the river. I'm in the humour for it, and I'll do it."

Nora Spruhan did not follow, and Richard O'Meara continued his way. He went direct for the cataracts so often spoken of; he walked into the water until it reached above his knees; and he stood there under the heaviest column of the falling water.

"You can see from this the very spot where he stood," said Michael, taking the Half-pay by the arm, and pointing downwards. "He stood on the shelf in the middle where the fall is sthrongest. I stole out afther him when he was going out; Lord be good to us, I took it into my head that he was for taking his life by throwing himself into a watery grave. I was afraid to go too near him; and if he did dash himself in what could I do? But I saw poor Teague, the dog, at his heels, and I knew that poor Teague wouldn't let him sink, and that between Teague and myself we'd save him. But he didn't do what I dreaded; and indeed, and indeed Curnel, if you were to see our poor honest dog keeping close to him as he waded into the river, and if you were to see the poor brute trying to look up at his master while the water was tumbling down direct into his eyes, you'd love our poor dog, and you couldn't help it."

After a while Richard O'Meara retraced his steps to his cottage. He made his way into an empty bedroom; drenched as he was he flung himself suddenly on the floor, and slept the heavy, uneasy sleep that renovates the drunkard for a fresh debauch.

CHAPTER XXVIII.

"FOLLOW THE LEADER."—THE COLONEL'S HAND AND WORD.

"I'LL bet a halfpenny you often played at 'follow the leader,' Curnel?" Michael Hanrahan asked; "that is, at the time when you were a small chap, and when your two natural legs only wanted the wind of the word to be off at full gallop. I'll engage you often played 'follow the leader' then, Curnel?"

"I did."

"Ah! isn't it the sporting play, Curnel? 'Hurroo!' says the leader, 'follow the leader, boys;' and off he goes at the top of his speed. 'Hurroo!' and away we are at his heels as fast as the legs can carry us. Up with him to the top of the cranky hill, like a crazy goat; up to the top of the cranky hill with every one of us, all crazy goats like him. Down tumbles the leader, down we all tumble too. Over, and over, and over, the leader rolls down to the bottom, along the slippery grass; over, and over, and over, we all roll down, taking patthern by him. And we knock against aich other, and roll over aich other, till we get to the bottom like him. Hurroo! up he is again, and away he goes; away *we* go, hot foot. There's no stepping-stones over the brook though; we must come to a halt! Whillaloo, my dear! he won't pull up. He shuts his fists, bends his back, and takes a canthering run at it, and over the brook he flies, clearing it from bank to bank. He is a tip-top leader, that he is. Hurroo! by the piper we'll have wet jackets. No matther, we can't be skulkers, we must 'follow the leader' to the off side. Over we go,—ha!—but four of the leaden-heels are in over head and ears, and sprawling at the bottom. 'Don't laugh, boys,' says the leader, ''tis a shame.' But he laughs his own self, and we all screech while the blinking, drowned rafts are pulling out. Naw bocklisch! off we are again, as fresh as ever. There's the leader making a big jump over nothing at all; by coorse, we must jump sky-high over the same. Now he's sitting atop of the style playing the bagpipes on his shin-bone, wagging his elbow to bring the wind into his chanther; we must squat there too, and play our tunes afther him. Och! there he is now, going up to the cow in the middle of the field, and making her a very mannerly bow, dragging down his poll by pulling at his forehead-lock; then he tugs her by the tail and makes off. The cow only waits for three mannerly bows, and three tugs at her tail; off she scuds, and the 'Paddy Lasts' can't overtake her. Hurroo, hurroo, hurroo! over hills, and into hollows with us; and in the long run we come to a standstill where the leader is sitting on the bench, undher the owld hawthorn at the Cross Roads. We were making a short cut from school all the while, and afther sitting down to dhraw breath a minute, every one takes his own way home. Och, Curnel! what a sporting play it is!"

While Michael described the "sporting play" of "follow the leader," he became quite excited. Carried away by the vivid recollection of his boyish days, there was a temporary forgetfulness of his special object. The excitement ceased with his subject, and his previous sobriety of manner returned.

"Curnel," he said,—"'follow the leader' is played by big men, when they aren't boys any longer. 'Follow the leader' is played by owld, shaky heads with white hair on them, and the greatest fool in the world can tell that 'tis 'follow the leader' into the churchyard and down into the grave."

The Half-pay, by a punch down of his cudgel, and an abrupt motion of his head, signified his credence in this philosophy. We doubt, however, if he was able to see the drift of its propounder, as it must be admitted that Michael took a rather roundabout road to his goal.

"Upon my word, and upon my conscience, Curnel, 'twasn't to be a back-biter or a dethractor

I came here to-day. The Heavens above knows it wasn't to let my tongue loose against our poor victim of a man. No, no,—Curnel!—I made known to you our sad state, and what brought us to our sad state for the reason,—that I want you to be our angel's friend,—to help her in her need. If you don't—mind what I say to you here face to face—in the land of the living she won't be long, and you'll be to blame."

The Half-pay never gave such an out-and-out flourish of the blackthorn as he did when Michael closed his appeal.

"I'll help!"—he barked forth.

"Well, the long and the short of it comes to this, Curnel. I came here to ask you for the love of God to play 'follow the leader' for us to the saving of our angel's life. That poor misguided fool of ours, Heaven help him, wouldn't be the way he is only for that same play. He wouldn't gallop at full speed, if he hadn't others to lead the way for him."

The Half-pay winced.

"Curnel, I might as well go whistle jigs to a milestone, thinking that it would dance the jig to the music, as to go to Ned Culkin, or to Tom O'Loughlin. Ned Culkin would shiver out of his skin, and his bones would fall asundher with the shaking if he stopped the dhrink. And Tom O'Loughlin would shrivel to a natomy if he didn't get the liquor. Mary and myself laid our heads together, and we said our only hope was in you, Curnel. 'Go to the bridge, between twelve and one o'clock,' says Mary, 'and you'll be sure to meet the Curnel. He'll be afther sleeping off the fumes of the night,' says she, 'and he'll be there to take in some fresh air afther the dhrinking.'"

The Half-pay winced again.

"'Go to the bridge, Michael,' says Mary to me. 'The Curnel dhrinks like a fish,' says Mary—"

The Half-pay shrugged his shoulders.

"'But,' says Mary, 'he's a good owld sowl for all that. Make your prayer to him,' says Mary. 'Petition him for the honour of God, and for the sake of our suffering angel, to give up the liquor himself—' "

"I'll drink—no more!"

"'And,' says Mary, 'beg and beseech of him that he'll turn away our poor crature of a man from the dhrink, as well as himself.' "

"He shall—drink—no more!"

"'We'll pray for him night and morning,' says Mary, 'and the childre will pray for him,' says Mary, 'if by his giving the example and the advice, he turns our crature of a man from the dhrink.' "

"I will."

"Your hand on it, Curnel."

"There."

"Well, Curnel," said Michael Hanrahan, shaking the hand he held, with a long continuous shake, "you'll have our prayers and our blessing, I promise you. And you'll be like the giver of a charity—you'll be joyful yourself."

CHAPTER XXIX.

THE COLONEL SETS ABOUT THE REFORMATION OF HIS CRONIES.

The past night had been, as Toby Purcell expressed it, "an out-and-out moist night." "A mighty, mighty, mighty happy, agreeable night," Tom O'Loughlin smilingly declared it to have been. "A night above all the nights," was Ned Culkin's estimate of it, as well as the chattering of his teeth would allow him to be heard. And so, it was later than usual when these two devotees to the "Irish Bacchus" emerged from their sleeping apartments.

When Michael Hanrahan had gone away, full of hope in the prosperity of his diplomacy, the Half-pay at once started off on a rapid promenade from one end of the bridge to the other. From time to time he came to a stand-still, and communed with himself. At each renewal of his hasty march, his leg and stick were delved down resolutely,—significant of firm determination. All the time that he so continued to hurry on and pause alternately,—his knotted brows had not relaxed, and the three deep furrows still radiated towards his beaver. Beyond yea or nay, the current of silent laughter generally circulating behind his lips did not flow.

Ned Culkin tottered forth from his little shabby-genteel house. Tom O'Loughlin thrust his head and neck through the glassless portion of his centre upper story, and having ascertained that the Half-pay was at the usual trysting-place, he hastened to join his neighbour, and both made their way downwards, Tom giving his assistance occasionally to the rickety little gauger.

The usual salutation having been exchanged between the three cronies,—

"Come, Curnel," and Ned Culkin sought his wonted matutinal support by leaning on the Half-pay's arm. "Come, Curnel," he chattered, "off we set at once for Joe Darmody's."

"To have our morning,—our cordial drop of brandy to revive us," grinningly assented Tom O'Loughlin.

"Damn—Joe!—Damn brandy!—damn whis—ky!—damn punch!—"

Such a continuous series of explosions had never been heard from the Half-pay's lips since his arrival in "The Town of the Cascades." As he blurted them forth, he snatched his arm from Ned Culkin, and the debilitated little man would have fallen had he not grasped the parapet of the bridge.

Next, the Half-pay started away as if pursued, down the descent of the bridge, and some distance further on.

"Thunder and ages!" shrieked out the astounded Ned Culkin. "What kind of humour is that he's in?—If I didn't let him loose, the arm was out of me!—Is it a joke?—or is he in earnest?—or is he in his senses?"

"Upon my faith, 'twould set me to say yes or no.

You could never tell his temper by looking at him. But I half think there's some tantrum on him. As long as I know him, and as often as I drank with him, I never heard him curse before. Oh, did you hear *how* he cursed? Whist!—here he comes back."

Back again did the Half-pay hasten. He halted suddenly in front of the cronies as they stood together.

"Damn—Joe—Dar—mody!"

And on he went as fast as before, in the opposite direction.

"He's gone crazy!" said Ned Culkin.

"There's something about him I never saw before," assented Tom O'Loughlin. "Whist! he's back again."

The Half-pay halted as before in his impetuous career.

"Damn—brandy!"

And again he hurried forward.

As he had done when Michael Hanrahan told of the blows given to "the angel," backward and forward the Half-pay hurried, as fast as though two good legs of bone and muscle had still upborne him, instead of one. And each time he came opposite his tippling companions, he had a fresh denunciation to make.

As he hurried to and fro, his wondering observers remarked that he frequently raised his beaver, and remained for a time bareheaded. At length, the inward motive power propelling him ceased apparently to work. He stopped short, fixed himself firmly at anchor, and glared from Ned Culkin to Tom O'Loughlin, and from Tom O'Loughlin to Ned Culkin as if he tendered to both his most resolute defiance.

Ned Culkin had not recovered the shaking his rickety frame had got when the Half-pay had so violently tugged away his arm, and he could do nothing but stare and shiver.

"He-he-he!" Tom O'Loughlin giggled; but there was a nervous misgiving in his manner as he added; "you're mighty humorous and uncommon pleasant in yourself this morning, Colonel."

"I'm—furious!"

"We'll be going, Tom," chattered Ned Culkin, and he secured the support of Tom's arm to help him on the way.

"With the best will in the world, Mr. Culkin. And our Colonel will come, I'm sure."

"No!"

The dissent was a bellow to make one jump.

"Well, well!" Tom O'Loughlin temporized in his blandest manner, "Mr. Culkin and myself will take our morning—"

"No!"

And effectually stopping their progress, the Half-pay stood.

"Drink—no more!" he vociferated, slapping his beaver, and driving it down to his ears, significant that he spoke for himself.

"Drink—no more—you!"

"Drink—no more—you!"—

And he pointed first to Ned Culkin, second to Tom O'Loughlin.

What?—could this be possible? To all appearance the Half-pay was in no jesting humour. But —phoo—phoo!—that he of all men was to enforce the doctrine of temperance, appeared to be a sheer impossibility. And yet there he stood, effectually barring the progress of the poor shivering gauger, and of the decayed gentleman, to Joe Darmody's—when, arm-in-arm, the blind leading the blind, they endeavoured to move wide of him, he still confronted them.

"Home—home!"

He commanded authoritatively. The two baffled tipplers were sorely puzzled.

"We'll soon see how it is," whispered Tom O'Loughlin to his friend. "Mr. O'Meara is coming up."

"Boozey in the night, and thirsty in the morning," Richard O'Meara said as he came up. He spoke hoarsely and discordantly; his lips were parched and scaly, his eyes blood-shot and sunken; his face was haggard, and there was ill-temper and discontent in his look and about his mouth. His attire was slovenly and soiled.

At the sound of his voice, the Half-pay bounced round and fixed his eyes sternly on him. The expression of the Half-pay's face being at all times ambiguous, Richard O'Meara observed no change in the inscrutable man. He passed on and joined the two others.

He stretched his arms, and yawned languidly.

"I'd take my oath of it," he said, with a sickly attempt at levity, "that the conscience of the fellow that drinks at night, dwells in his stomach. If the stomach does not preach to him, there is no self-accusation. But 'a hair of the same hound' is a classical proverb, a thousand years old at least,—just as true in the land of potatoes as in ancient Rome. So, to quiet conscience, let us have a hair of the same hound down at Joe Darmody's or anywhere else."

"He, he, he! we were just on the road," giggled Tom O'Loughlin.

"On then, in double quick time. Right about face, and head the march, Colonel."

"I won't!" snarled the Half-pay.

"But I say you must, my honest fellow. Come along, man, come along." And he grasped the Half-pay's arm in a friendly manner. The Half-pay jirked away Richard O'Meara's hand, and pushed him back with all his force—no puny strength.

"Drink – no—more!" he shouted forth, as Richard O'Meara staggered from him.

"What—what's the meaning of this?" Richard O'Meara demanded in astonishment.

"You—scoundrel!" roared the Half-pay, "you—poltroon!—you—struck—your—angel—wife!"

Richard O'Meara started as if he had been suddenly pierced by some sharp instrument.

"Rascal!—scoun-drel!—pol-troon!—Drink—no—more!"

And, as in his own fashion, the Half-pay fulfilled his engagement with Michael Hanrahan of turning the husband of the "angel" from his drinking habits, he flourished his cudgel fiercely, to give due effect to his abrupt and abusive expostulation.

Ned Culkin or Tom O'Loughlin could no

longer mistake the point-blank nature of his sentiments.

"And why have you dared," Richard O'Meara asked, in a hoarse, inward voice, "to meddle in my private concerns? Why have you dared to play the spy on my family affairs?"

As he spoke he approached the Half-pay, it was evident, with no friendly intent.

"Ras-cal! — scoun-drel! — pol-troon! — You—struck—your—an-gel—wife!—Drink—no—more!"

Much more rapidly than the words were uttered——these came only at intervals—did the reformer's cudgel descend about the head and shoulders of the man he would reform. He was redeeming his pledge to Michael Hanrahan with a vengeance. If there be indeed "sermons in stones," the Half-pay was seemingly of opinion that a blackthorn cudgel could preach an effectual sermon on the evils of intemperance.

He was grappled by the throat and by the arm. He was a stalwart man, but he was a pigmy in Richard O'Meara's gripe.

"I will not return your blows, you mad cripple," said his captor, as he shook him and lifted him from the ground; "but I'll fling you over the bridge to cool you."

It is not at all improbable but that this threat, delivered through the clenched teeth of the threatener, would have been carried into effect. But timely interference was at hand.

People flock together as some birds do. When one alights, another, soaring on speedy wing sees a bird of fellow plumage below him. He curbs his onward progress, and circling downwards folds his wings and stands beside his brother. Another and another whirl down, no doubt surmising that something important or attractive is in hand. And so there is a congregation; and as the numbers augment, the quicker do aërial voyagers descend to join them.

Thus it was on the bridge of the cascades. The personal scuffle between the Half-pay and Richard O'Meara arrested the passengers. And as the crowd increased, and loud voices were heard, people hurried from the town, and ran fast lest they should be late for the altercation.

At the foot of the bridge nearest the town there was a small house, the lower story of which was occupied by shoemakers. As the racers to the bridge went by, the shoemakers stared out. They questioned each other as to the cause of the scampering by their window, and then they too set off, convinced, like the birds, that something worth attending to was in agitation.

These shoemakers, every man and boy of them, were intimates of the Half-pay. For years he had turned in daily to stare at them, to say "Maw—maw!" and little more. But they were attached to him in consequence of his daily visits.

These friendly shoemakers rescued the Half-pay from the peril brought on by his too ardent missionary spirit. As he stood encircled by them, as his body-guard, Richard O'Meara, Ned Culkin, and Tom O'Loughlin walked away into the town together. They did not proceed to Joe Darmody's;—they turned short into the widow-woman's "Entertainment," and there sought the privacy of the "lone room."

The result of their conference therein will be learned further on.

Alack and well-a-day! for the carefully devised plan of Michael Hanrahan and his counsellor and sweetheart, Mary.

CHAPTER XXX.

THE HALF-PAY FURTHER PROVES HIS ZEAL, AND EXCITES HIS NEIGHBOURS.

While in the widow-woman's "lone room" Ned Culkin was eagerly replenishing his system with a fresh supply of caloric to replace that which had so rapidly radiated into the cool morning air—while the decayed gentleman was elevating himself from his beggarly condition, to a forgetfulness of what he had been, and what he was—and while the degraded Richard O'Meara was restoring his unstrung nerves to the unnatural tension they had of late been forced to,—and the three were engaged commenting on the inexplicable conduct of the Half-pay, the object of their discourse was seen stumping through the main street of "The Town of the Cascades," along which he hurried with unprecedented velocity.

His midday walk through the main street had been heretofore a leisurely promenade, no business on hand requiring haste. To be sure, his discourse was curt and scanty, but his salutation of "Maw—maw," was frequent; his shake of the hand with this or that neighbour was hearty, at times over-hearty, the owner of the hand wincing from the violence of the pressure, while his salutes to those less intimate, and to the fair sex particularly, were constant.

On the present occasion he pressed onward at the top of his speed, looking neither to the right nor left, noticing no one. He went with his head thrown back, and he stared directly before him, at something above the elevation of his eyes; something discernible to his mental vision.

A rumour had spread through "The Town of the Cascades" of some *mêlée* on the bridge, in which the Colonel had been the principal actor. Much excitement prevailed in consequence, and people were all alive examining each other as to the nature and extent of the scuffle that had taken place. So that when the reputed hero of the fight was seen hurrying onward as described, he became an object of eager scrutiny and speculation.

Nick Mahaffy was standing at his shop-door, his stumpy legs wide apart, and both his hands thrust deep into his waistcoat pockets. The Half-pay took no more notice of Nick Mahaffy than if he were a nonentity, and not the head man of the town. Nick Mahaffy took two straddling steps from his door into the street, and knitting his brows, and pursing his lips, he gazed haughtily, and with ruffled dignity, after the uncourteous passer-by. Paddy Dreelan, Nick Mahaffy's satellite, came forth, because Nick Mahaffy had come forth, and he strained his neck to look after the hurrying Half-pay, because Nick Mahaffy looked after him.

Toby Purcell was lolling against the door jambs of the "McMahon Arms" (Toby's hotel was seldom over-thronged), and Toby, a cynical leer playing round his mouth and glancing from his eyes, stooped forward to scan the progress of the hurrying Colonel, who passed him without the slightest recognition.

Paddy Dreelan crossed over to Nick Mahaffy; and Toby Purcell joined them. And others came; and there was a knot,—all eyes in the knot following the motions of the Half-pay.

On went the Half-pay without abatement of speed, on, nearly to the termination of the main street. Sharp he turned to the left, into a lane or *cul-de-sac*, entered, as one of the aborigines described it, "through a square archway;" that is to say, the houses on either side were continued above the entrance, so that the entrance was not through an archway at all. Half a dozen small houses were in this lane, and it was called "Bow-lane," why so called no one could tell me, and there was no sign of bow or arrow in its locale, to direct my conjectures.

"Ha!—by the piper that played before Moses," suggested Toby Purcell, "he's going to Paddy Gow to have the leg scoured out, and put in shooting order. And if there doesn't be murther, then I'm a false prophet."

This shrewd guess put forth by Toby Purcell requires explanation.

Paddy Gow, or Paddy the smith, lived in Bow-lane, entered from the main street through the "square archway." The Cyclopean breathing of Paddy Gow's bellows, the roaring of Paddy Gow's forge-fire, and the din of Paddy Gow's anvil monopolized the entire resonance of Bow-lane beyond the "square archway." Paddy Gow was the cunning artificer who had prepared the blunderbuss-barrel as a substitute for part of the Half-pay's original wooden leg. This proof of Paddy Gow's skill as a worker in metals was generally known, and hence Toby Purcell's assertion was not without a groundwork of probability.

As suddenly as he had been lost to view, the Half-pay emerged from Bow-lane, passing of course again under the "square archway." Over his left shoulder, the handle grasped firmly in his right hand, he carried a good-sized sledge-hammer; not Paddy Gow's large sledge, which required two sinewy arms to wield it, but Paddy Gow's half-and-half—between his hammer and his two-handed sledge.

"Oh!—by the powers of pewter!" ejaculated Toby Purcell; "if he isn't going to sledge somebody's skull, I'm a jack-snipe."

"The man is stark mad. I insist on it; he's stark mad," dictated Nick Mahaffy.

"Upon my word and credit," assented Paddy Dreelan, sententiously and impressively, "he has the look of a crature that took leave of his senses."

There were other apt commentaries which I have not time now to notice.

The person so critically scrutinized rapidly approached. To judge from the line of forced march he was pursuing it was his intention to keep wide of his assembled neighbours. When within a pace or two he diverged from his course, as if a sudden squall had taken him aback, and right through the group of observers did he dash. To the utter consternation of Paddy Dreelan, he came full tilt against the short, burly Nick Mahaffy, who was too inactive, and indeed too dignified, to jump to one side as the others had done, and but for the timely aid of Paddy the important Nick Mahaffy would have been overturned. It was the conclusion, however, that the offender had been rude without intention;—Nick Mahaffy and his companions had not been observed by him, it was supposed, his gaze being fixed on some aërial object at a considerable elevation, and at a distance.

"'Twas a narrow escape I had," whispered Toby Purcell; "the iron leg was within an inch of my toes."

"What is he about at all?" queried one of the lookers-on, whispering, as Toby Purcell had done.

"Whatever he's on for," Toby Purcell answered, "there's fun in him—that I'd swear for. He has the wag in his head,—the only sign of humour about him at any time."

And Toby Purcell was right. There was a characteristic vibration of the Half-pay's head, and this motion was produced now, as at other times, by the effort to suppress the silent laughter he indulged in whenever it circulated with increased velocity. The Half-pay knew right well he had succeeded in taxing the sagacity of the group he had, not undesignedly, disturbed. And this knowledge was sufficient to make him forget for a while his previous sternness.

"Come here, Jack."

Toby Purcell addressed one of those tatterdemalions to be found in every part of Ireland where there is an inn or house of "entertainment," or a public vehicle of any kind, who issue forth in the morning without any particular object in view;—who spend nearly the entire day lolling listlessly in thoroughfares and at corners;—who are remarkable for keenness of eye and accuracy of observation;—and who spring at once into energy and briskness when any chance employment offers.

"Jack, do you see the Colonel?"

"Ha, ha!—I do, Misther Purcell, I do. To be sure I do."

"Jack, do you see that there's a sledge-hammer over the Colonel's shoulder?"

"Ha, ha!—I see the sledge-hammer plain,

Misther Purcell. The sight of my eyes is good, Misther Purcell, Lord be praised."

"Go now, Jack, and don't lose sight of the Colonel. Bring word to us here where he goes to, and what he does with himself and the sledge-hammer. We'll wait here for you, Jack. Mind your points now."

Jack made no bargain as to recompense. Jack always preferred to undertake a job without compact; he relied on his powers of persuasion when his mission had been fulfilled. Jack had a deformed foot, and he progressed by a series of jumps, the stick that aided him being in front of his person. Jack pulled the peak of his remnant of a cap by way of salutation, and hopped off on his errand.

Fifteen minutes or so might have elapsed when the knot of inquisitors, so athirst for intelligence, observed Jack returning. He came at his top speed;—he could hop marvellously fast, every bone and muscle twisting as he hopped. I shall give the result of his "*reconnaissance*" in his own words. I should however remark, that Jack paused at every sentence of his narrative, that each distinct occurrence might be impressed the more strongly on his hearers, and be the more fully appreciated.

"Over the bridge the Colonel went."—A pause.

"And he crossed the bridge. I seen him crossing over with my two eyes."—Pause.

"Up he climbed, the poor man, and hard set he was, the poor man. An' he climbed until he stud fornent the dure of his own house. You know where his own house is, Misther Purcell? I b'lieve ye all know where the Curnel's house is, gentlemen?"—Pause.

"When he was before the dure of his own house, gentlemen, he put his stick between his knees this way—this way."

"He has but one knee," remarked Toby Purcell.

"I think he has two. No matther—he put the stick this way; an' he lifted down the sledge-hammer from his shoulder with his two hands. You may b'lieve me; I'm not telling a word of lie. I was leaning over the bridge looking up at him. I was, gentlemen; 'tis the thruth I'm tellin'."—Pause.

"'Ha, ha!' says I to myself, 'by this an' by that, he's goin' to make pipe stoppers of the dure.'"—Pause.

"Did he—did he make pipe-stoppers of it?" The question was impatiently put.

"Wait till I tell ye. He laid the sledge-hammer down by his feet—"

"He has but one foot."

"Oh, sure enough, thin, Misther Purcell, you're right. He *has* but one fut, the poor man. Well, he laid the sledge-hammer down by his one fut—an' he tuk up his stick, an' he malleted at the dure till you'd think he'd smash it. I wondher you didn't hear the noise down here, he malleted so hard."—Pause.

"He malleted an' he malleted until the dure was pulled wide open."—Pause.

"An' he lifted up the sledge-hammer, he did, no doubt about it. An' he put it on his shouldher again. An' he—went in over the threshold. An' the dure was shut out—with a bang—that shuck the bridge I was standing on."

"Is that all you saw, Jack?"

"That's all, gentlemen; that's all."

And so, the laudable thirst for information felt so keenly by the inquisitors of "The Town of the Cascades" was still unslaked.

CHAPTER XXXI.

WHAT THE COLONEL WAS DOING IN HIS OWN HOUSE.

The three tipplers, Ned Culkin, Tom O'Loughlin, and our friend the Half-pay were three bachelors, irresponsible for any one but themselves. And so much the better.

In this respect they were less morally blameable than their late adherent Richard O'Meara, who had desecrated the altars of his household gods. Neither Ned Culkin, nor Tom O'Loughlin, nor the Half-pay had household gods to build altars for. And so they had no household altars in their half-dilapidated little houses.

The three tippling bachelors were economical in their way. Ned Culkin was economical, because, out of every five shillings he could reckon on, four never entered the house at all. Tom O'Loughlin was economical from sheer necessity;—no one could extract money from an empty purse. The Half-pay was domestically economical for reasons best known to himself;—which reasons the ablest miners in "The Town of the Cascades" were unable to bring to the surface.

I have given the three neighbours due credit for their domestic saving. One evidence thereof I adduce, and the circumstance will also prove the friendly terms on which they lived.

The three tippling bachelors had come to the understanding that one elderly woman, Bridget Scallon by name, was sufficient to discharge the household duties of all three. Bridget Scallon was a widow beyond her fortieth year. She was blear eyed; no one could fault her on this account, her hours for regular sleep being but few. She was slovenly in her dress;—no wonder again,—what time could she devote to her toilette with her three separate establishments to attend to? She wore shoes and stockings on Sunday only;—so much the better; she could race from house to house more nimbly with bare feet than if those feet were encumbered.

My friend, Mary Hanrahan, in her own vein of quiet humour, gave me an insight into the arrangements of the tipplers, under favour of which the wiry, but ever scrambling and grumbling Bridget Scallon succeeded in serving three masters.

"'Twas aisy enough," she said, "to plaze the gauger. A dhrink of cool wather from the spring was a hearty breakfast to him, an' he'd snap up a few mouthfuls by way of a dinner, any time he got it;—a chop of mutton well scalded with pepper and salt, or a pig's crubeen, half salt, didn't take much time in the cooking. The half of a penny bun, and a little cup of milk, was the decayed gentleman's breakfast; the other half of the penny bun, with a couple of eggs or a salt herring, gave him a grand dinner. The gauger, Michael told me, was, like the woodcock, nourished on the dhrink; he said the woodcocks lived all out on bog water, and the gauger on the liquor. The decayed gentleman would have stood his own friend betther in the way of ating if he could get credit anywhere through the town, but, for the most part, if he was to turn his pockets inside out 'twould be no gains to him. The Curnel was the only one of Bridget's three masthers that took care of himself. Very sthrong tea—very sthrong tea entirely—he'd have in the mornin', an', for *both* their sakes, Bridget made it to his liking. 'Twas the tea that kept Bridget awake and lively for twenty hours out of the twenty-four, and the Curnel's teapot was her best friend. When it was getting weak, she towld me, poor woman, a dhrop of spirits out of the gauger's bottle or the Curnel's bottle made it as sthrong as ever,—and there was no scarcity of that with the gauger or the Curnel. Three eggs the Curnel scooped clean out every morning with his sthrong tea, and his half loaf; and then Bridget had no more to provide for him. His dinner came cooked to him from the widow-woman's. Not one of Bridget's three masthers minded about cobwebs, or dust, or anything that way, and she lost little time cleaning or sweeping. So you see, with the help of the sthrong tea, seasoned from the bottle, poor Bridget was able to meet all calls."

Between three and four o'clock the day of the rencounter on the bridge, Tom O'Loughlin gave three modest taps at the Half-pay's door. I have said this door was knockerless;—the knocker was indeed gone, but the iron knob belonging to it remained. With a stone suitable for his purpose, Tom O'Loughlin struck this knob. A plebeian, seeking admittance, would have given a vigorous single bang; a fellow with money in his pocket—Nick Mahaffy, for instance—might claim attention by a resounding tantarare. Tom O'Loughlin was not a plebeian, and as far as money was concerned, —*that* was out of the question. So he temporized by tapping the knob timidly three times.

Bridget Scallon blinked her inflamed eyes at him as she answered his summons.

"I'm nothing beyond the relics of a harassed

owld woman," she whined, "one pulling me one way, another, another way, the night as well as the day, all the same. There isn't as much for you as a scrap that would lie in a fippeny-piece."

"I have dined, Bridget."

"The more your luck. I hadn't a crumb for you."

"I came to speak to the Colonel, Bridget. He is within, I believe?"

"Within he is, but what to make of his doings is to me a mysthery."

"What are they, Bridget?"

"'Tis perplexin' my owld brain. Seein' is b'lievin', they say,—but until I see it I won't give in to it. Of all the men that ever breathed the breath of life, for him to do it!—"

"What, Bridget?"

"I don't suppose,"—Bridget spoke rather in soliloquy,—"that the priest that goes about layin' his curse on the liquor would bring himself to do it. No, he wouldn't be guilty of the like. But to think that the Curnel would commit sich a deadly mortal sin!—I won't b'lieve it till I see it; no, I won't."

"Hallo, hallo!"

It was the Half-pay's stentorian bellow that caused Bridget Scallon to jump round, and scamper inward, leaving Tom O'Loughlin bewildered by her unfinished communication.

In the all but nude little parlour off the hall, the creeping Tom found his neighbour. The sledge-hammer that had caused such perplexity to the group of inquisitors in the main street was on the floor, and leaning against the wall was the blackthorn that had so naïvely begun the reformation of Richard O'Meara.

The Half-pay had put down the sledge-hammer, and placed the blackthorn at rest, to enable him to use both hands in the work he was engaged at. Bridget Scallon was bent nearly double, and her master Number One was in the act of depositing on her back a goodly-sized keg, which, to judge by the exertion required on her part, and also by the exclamation forced out from Bridget, as it was fixed, not over-gently, in its position, was a weighty keg as well as a good sized one.

With great energy and despatch the Half-pay, holding the keg in its place with one hand, gathered up the carrier's old gown, and therewith formed an *appui* for her burthen, by passing it over her shoulder, fixing it in her clutch, and riveting her fingers on it. He then stepped back from her, and contemplated his work with entire satisfaction. He grasped his cudgel, he took up the sledge-hammer, and flung it across his shoulder.

"Trot!" he barked.

And Bridget, obedient to the command, wheeled round, and did trot. She was obliged to proceed, however, in her bent position. It was plain to understand she must break down if her journey were a lengthened one.

"Maw!" said the Half-pay, recognizing Tom O'Loughlin's presence. "Come." And he hastened on as Bridget Scallon's escort.

Out into the little yard behind the shabby-genteel house did the tottering Bridget trot. There was a bench in this little yard, overshadowed with trees. On this bench the Half-pay used to lounge at times to smoke his pipe. There was a partial view of the river from this resting-place; it looked directly towards the hill-top churchyard noticed in our early Chapters. There was a glimpse of the town too, and the dash of the water below the bridge was heard. In truth it was a pleasant spot for a lounge and a smoke.

This bench Bridget, of her own accord, approached. She wheeled round and sat down, and uttering a moan of relief, rested the keg on it. The Half-pay hastened over, and assisted her to fix it there firmly.

Arranged three deep, to the right and left of the bench, was a goodly company of black bottles, sealed and corked. These had been ranged in military array, so that when Bridget's fardel had taken its prominent position, the bottles had all the appearance of a guard attendant on it.

The Half-pay, shouldering his sledge-hammer,

wheeled quickly round and confronted Tom O'Loughlin. He gave his composite leg a resolute punch downwards, delving the ferruled end of his cudgel into the ground at the same time. He looked straight into the eyes of his neighbour, with even more than usual intensity, and beyond yea or nay the interior cachinnation in which he frequently indulged was in excess, and flowed in a brisk current.

"Hallo!" he cried. And the hallo! from its suddenness and vigour, startled Tom O'Loughlin, to whom it was addressed.

With the reader's permission, I will give the Half-pay's thoughts in words, as they passed rapidly his mind.

"All preliminaries are arranged so far," he informed himself; "well arranged—all ready for assault. I took my oath to that good-hearted poor fellow, Michael Hanrahan, that liquor of any shape should never pass down my throat again. And the oath I'll keep."

At this point of his mental colloquy with himself leg and stick were delved down.

"I engaged to Michael that I would compel others to lead as sober a life as myself. And this engagement also I'll keep—or I'll know for what."

Here his thoughts diverged; the stream of interior cachinnation was unsluiced, and eddied and whirled in a rapid stream.

"Ha, ha!—I have bewildered the wits of the whole town to-day. Ha, ha!—ho, ho! What in the name of heaven could the Colonel, as they have named me, want with the sledge-hammer he carried on his shoulders? Ha, ha! ho, ho!—ho, ho! Bridget Scallon thinks her Colonel is a bedlamite. Ho, ho! And if this unfortunate fellow here is not perplexed at my movements, I'm a colonel in downright earnest. Ha, ha!—ho, ho, ho! I know well what he's come for. But I am ready to keep my promise to Michael Hanrahan—as he shall see."

CHAPTER XXXII.

THE DUEL.

In answer to the "hallo!" that had made him bound, Tom O'Loughlin proceeded to discharge his mission. I should remark that the decayed gentleman's manner was much altered during his present conference with the Half-pay. Somewhat of the spirit and demeanour of his early days returned to him,—of those days when he was a pleasant, hearty fellow, with money to waste, and no prevoyance of future pauperism.

"I come on a rather unpleasant business, Colonel," he said.

"What?"

"This day, Colonel,—I regret I was there to

witness it,—you publicly degraded our mutual friend, Mr. Richard O'Meara."

"Whaled him—well?"

"You struck him with your stick, on the public bridge of this town."

"He'll get—more—if—" the Half-pay did not finish this sentence.

"It is scarcely necessary for me to say, Colonel, that a public insult of this nature must be as publicly acknowledged and apologized for,—or the offending party must—"

"Fight?"

Tom O'Loughlin bowed, and then looked at the Half-pay with an air by no means cringing.

"As the friend of Mr. O'Meara, Colonel, I am here to require that you will make a public apology for the public insult given."

"Won't!"

"Then, Colonel, it only remains for me to act as Mr. Richard O'Meara's friend. I have not the honour, Colonel, of knowing your name, I presume you will have no objection to give it me?"

"Name—is—"

While pronouncing these words the Half-pay whirled round; he allowed his cudgel to fall, and wielded the sledge-hammer with both hands.

"*Paddy*—WHACK!" he shouted. And at the word "Whack," which surname he assumed for the occasion, he stove in the head of the keg Bridget Scallon had placed on the bench.

"Paddy—Whack!" he continued to shout out. And at every repetition of the euphonious surname, he dealt his blows vigorously on the body-guard of black bottles—until not one remained unbroken.

From keg and bottles a united stream of potteen flowed about the yard, thence into the sewer, and from the sewer into the river. The atmosphere was redolent with the stinging effluvia of potteen;—and Toby Purcell assured me that the water of the river was converted into grog, and that an angler then engaged in his pastime filled his pannier in a twinkling, so heedless and giddy had the fish become by the influence of the admixture. "In fact," Toby

Purcell affirmed, "the trouts became royally drunk, every one of them."

The astonishment, the more than astonishment of Tom O'Loughlin and Bridget Scallon was excessive. It was a mingled sensation of horror and grief that overwhelmed them. The grief of both was however thoroughly selfish. Tom O'Loughlin looked on with a melancholy visage while the inspiriting principle of his existence, that raised him nightly from his shivering sense of pauperism to forgetfulness and spreeishness, was wantonly wasted. And Bridget Scallon saw with a sad heart the never-failing strengthener of her tea gurgling away,—if we take Toby Purcell's authority, to tipsify the fishes.

"Oh, Colonel, Colonel," said Tom O'Loughlin, "you have destroyed——"

"The Devil!—Not—drunk—again,—you—he!"

And the Half-pay pointed in the direction of Richard O'Meara's cottage. Tom O'Loughlin sighed deeply.

"Well, well, Colonel!—permit me now to finish the affair that has brought me here. You decline to apologize?"

"I do."

"Then be good enough to refer me to a friend with whom I may arrange the preliminaries of the meeting. Who is to be your friend, Colonel, for the occasion?"

"Your—self!"

"Colonel! I am here as Mr. O'Meara's friend. It would give me pleasure to discharge the like duty for you on another occasion. But, as you perceive, I cannot do so now."

"Must!"

"Oh, Colonel, permit me to point out to you—"

"Won't!—Stay."

The Half-pay hastened off. From a compartment of his mysterious portmanteau he took out, carefully covered in woollen casings, two long-barrelled pistols, linked together by a strap. These he flung across his shoulder. From the same receptacle he extracted a small powder flask, having a bottom to screw off, in which were bullets and caps. Thus provided for, he presented himself before Richard O'Meara's friend.

"Ready?" he shouted.

As a matter of course, Tom O'Loughlin declined to be a party to such precipitancy. Nor would he consent to fill the part of second to the challenged as well as to the challenger. The Half-pay insisted on it, however, and the decayed gentleman departed to consult his principal.

Richard O'Meara, not free from the excitement of drink, and yet determined, as he professed, "to send the disabled old ruffian home on a door, stiff and stark," was tickled by the oddity of the Colonel's proposal, and he also decided that Tom O'Loughlin should discharge the unprecedented office in the history of duelling, of a go-between to both combatants. Tom, for good reasons of his own, had no mind to come to a misunderstanding with either, and so he finally agreed.

The sun, not yet risen from his couch, was but

glancing upwards with eyes half open, when Richard O'Meara, accompanied by the decayed gentleman, was on his way to the "sod." The spot selected was, in this instance, misnamed "a sod," there being no sod whatever. The rencounter, from which the Half-pay was to be "sent home stiff and stark," was to take place beyond the "village of the Bornochs," close by the sea-side, on a strip of smooth sandy beach. The battle-ground was chosen because of its seclusion, the affair being conducted with the greatest privacy, that the deadly intent of the challenger might not be interrupted.

The decayed gentleman and his original principal had but partially slept off the previous night's debauch, and they blinked like owls overtaken by the light of day. The little sandy beach they had to gain was more than two Irish miles distant from "The Town of the Cascades." It was yet grey morning when they reached it. Even at that very early hour, there stood the Half-pay, as erect, and as immovable as a post.

Over his shoulders hung his pistols, still in their

cases; and he had provided himself with a flat stone on which the muzzle of his leg rested, to prevent it from sinking into the yielding sand.

"The Colonel is no flincher, I see," Richard O'Meara carelessly remarked. "The quicker we proceed to business the better."

Tom O'Loughlin was soon busy as the manager of the performance. He shook the Half-pay's hand warmly, in answer to his salutation of "Maw, maw!" He loaded the Half-pay's pistols with the skill of a veteran duellist. Scanning the ground with experienced eye, he saw that his principal Number Two was unfavourably placed; there was a rock behind him that imparted too much of the character of a target to the present object of his arrangement. The Half-pay removed without objection to a fitter position. As he went along his leg sunk deep, and with some difficulty he drew it up at every step. Tom O'Loughlin did not fail to appreciate the utility of the flat stone, and he adjusted it as before. Tom O'Loughlin proved by his conduct that he was the soul of honour and fair duelling, and were such decayed gentlemen available on all similar occasions, I see no necessity why one person more than is really necessary should be engaged to arrange a duelling rencounter.

Taking the Half-pay as his starting post, Tom stepped twelve paces, an exact yard to each pace. It was not his first essay, and he could step three feet accurately. At twelve paces distant from the Half-pay, Tom placed his principal Number One.

The Second, or, more properly in this instance, the Third, was of course to give the word and make the signal for attack. He retired somewhat out of the range of bullets.

"Ready—Present—Fire!" he cried, in a loud, distinct voice, and he dropped his glove.

Either both had fired at the exact same instant, or there had been but one shot. Tom glanced from combatant to combatant. They both stood erect; neither faltered. He saw the Half-pay hastily raise his hand to his cheek, look at it, and then flourish his cudgel above his head. Tom subsequently discovered that the ball from Richard O'Meara's weapon had passed so close to his opponent's jaw, that a gap, marking its course, was cut through the umbrageous whisker that covered it. The Half-pay had barely escaped his threatened fate of being sent home on a door.

Startled by the report of the pistol, the gulls in a neighbouring cliff flew about screaming. One more inquisitive and bolder than the others came sailing over the head of Tom O'Loughlin's principal Number One. The Half-pay raised his arm rapidly and fired. The bird fell dead at Richard O'Meara's feet. Little doubt could there be that had the same bullet been sped against his opponent, the Half-pay would not have been the party doomed "to go home on a door."

The duel, according to all the laws of honour, so called, was terminated. The Half-pay had stood the fire of his opponent, and had not returned it.

And so, neither of the decayed gentleman's principals went home "on a door."

So far it will be seen that the plan of Michael Hanrahan and his Mary had been productive of little good result.

CHAPTER XXXIII.

THE DROOPING FLOWER.

"GOODNESS gracious knows," said Mary Hanrahan, clasping her hands within each other, placing them before her chest, rocking her person, and speaking in a plaintive tone—

"Goodness gracious knows, Michael an' myself supposed we were a pair of Solomons. We thought that if the Curnel turned from his dhrinking, that his example would work wondhers. We knew that our poor man had a mighty liking entirely for the Curnel, an' 'twas the thought of our wiseacre heads that the Curnël would coax him to play 'follow the leader,' as Michael called it. It never once came across our minds—how could it?—that he'd begin to convert our poor gone astray man by whacking him with his heavy stick. No, no. Such a notion never came near either of us."

Mary paused, and reflected for a moment. Her face had been serious and somewhat sad. The expression relaxed, and when she spoke again there was a tendency to a smile about her mouth and eyes.

"Michael an' myself were young," she said, "an' 'tis visible to me now we hadn't the sense we thought we had. I was quite certain, an' I wouldn't have b'lieved the priest to the conthrary, that my poor Michael couldn't go asthray. An' Michael was all out as certain that Mary, myself you know, was a patthern of wisdom. Indeed we were both in the wrong, as you can't help thinking, I'm sure.—An' I'll tell you what," she added, her smile becoming more positive, "I'm greatly inclined to think that from that day to this, the stock of sense we raked together between us wouldn't make a stack in our haggart. But for all that, we were as loving, an' as proud of our harvest, thanks be to God, as if we were wiser an' richer people.

"We were downright certain—Michael an' myself—when we laid our heads together, that we were doing all for the best—goodness gracious knows we were! But I'm grieved to tell you—"

Her smile faded away, and her sad look returned—

"I'm grieved to tell you that 'twas the mischief, an' not the good we brought about. Our poor deluded man went on worser an' worser from the moment the Curnel's stick welted his shouldhers. With fury in his eyes, an' with a loud, angry tongue, he spoke to our darling. He called her by ugly names, an' he told her she had made complaints of him to sthrangers, an' joined his enemies against him. When she fell on her knees before him, as white as the whitest linen, an' shivering like the leaves of the aspen three, he said to her that she was a liar, an' a thraitor to him. Poor soul!—you'd pity her if there was a heart of stone within you. Indeed you would—pity her."

The tears fell fast along Mary's cheeks at the recollection of what she described.

"Day by day she pined away and dhrooped. She cried herself to sleep in the night, an' she cried off an' on all the day. Oh!—you'd pity her! an' little wondher that she cried herself to sleep; little wondher that the tears came out undher the eyelids, along her cheeks, when they were closed in the sleep of wearisomeness! Often and often I saw them bursting out, an' wiped them away, as I sat watching by her. Little wondher it was—an' I didn't wondher at it—that the sad moans came from her aching bosom while she lay dozing! Her starts of sleep were short,—an' small wondher did I make of it, when she'd waken herself with the sound of her own lamentations, an' throw her arms round my neck, an' fell to crying again.

"The Lord be merciful to her soul! She had real cause to be sorrowful! If 'twas a thing there was no scalding of the heart, from the loss of her poor deluded husband's love an' tendherness, there was enough of other sorrow around her heart. Our little baby died!—our darling couldn't nurse him, an' he died! An' then the other child,—a little girl it was of two years old,—died too. Two more beautiful, wax-work little things you couldn't see. There was a month from the death of the one to the death of the other. Surely—surely our darling had cause for sorrow!"

"How did their father seem to take their death, Mary?"

"I saw that he was frightened; but he only drank the harder,—to dhrown his thoughts, Michael said it was. The Lord forgive him!—for he's gone before his Judge! May he be merciful to him, for he was a good poor fellow afther all, if it wasn't for the dhrink.

"All in my power I did to soothe an' comfort our sufferer. She'd listen without saying one word; —an' she'd cry—cry—cry! In her brightest days our darling was not sthrong or sturdy. She was delicate in her body; an' she was like a bird, merry an' blithesome, but fearful in herself an' shy. 'Twas easy to startle her and terrify her. 'Twas plain to see she couldn't hold out against her sorrow. Day by day she drooped an' pined away.

"'Tis my belief," said Mary, after a pause, "'tis my belief the tendherest heart—the heart that has the love the deepest—is the easiest to be broken. I know there are women in the world that would rise up against ill-usage, and pay it back to the giver. *I*'d do that, I think: I think I would. I give thanks I never got cause to stand up for my self,—no, never,—but I think I'd do it. But our darling was not one of my sort, an' the heart broke within her."

Mary ceased speaking. She clasped her hands very tightly, and the rocking of her person became continuous. She closed her eyes, her lips moved, and for some time it appeared to me that she was praying inaudibly.

After a considerable pause, she opened her eyes, sighed deeply, but remained silent.

"Your story is a sad one, Mary."

"Isn't it now, Sir, very, very sad?"

"Indeed it is."

There was another pause.

CHAPTER XXXIV.

SORE AND PLEASANT RETROSPECTIONS.

"How did the unhappy victim of intemperance behave to Michael?" I asked of Mary.

Mary sighed again—a lengthened sigh—before she answered me.

"Ah, then, indeed they went on bad enough together. Michael was forced to be hiding the most of the day, out of his sight entirely. The poor 'victim of intemperance,' I think you called him?"

I nodded assent.

"An' a good name it is to give him. The poor victim was dangerous to meet with often. He forgot all Michael's care of him, and Michael's love for him!—he did indeed. Ah, then, it often made me wondher. Many a time did I turn it over in my mind, without being able to find out a downright reason for it at all. You're a man that got a reasonable share of schooling, if I'm not greatly astray in my reckoning?"

"I did, Mary; a reasonable share of schooling, as you say."

"Ah! so I thought. An' I see myself, you have more of the world's craft in you than Michael or I had,—or ever will have, if we were to put both our shares together."

Mary's usual smile partly returned as she paid me this compliment.

"Thank you, Mary, for your high opinion of me."

"Who knows but you could explain to me how it came to pass that our unhappy victim, as you called him, showed a greater dislike to those he had the love for, than he had for sthrangers he didn't care a rush for? How did it happen that to our darling, an' to his childre, an' to his fosther-brother that doated on him, he was cross an' hard-hearted; an' for all that he could laugh, and shout out, and sing with such ones as the shivering gauger an' the decayed gentleman? Often an' often it perplexed me to undherstand this. Who knows but that you, with your schooling an' your world's wisdom, can unriddle it for me?"

Mary's question, although apparently paradoxical, was not profound; yet it created a necessity for reflection.

Mary awaited my reply.

"Mary, have you heard it said that people scarcely ever forgive those they have injured, although they may forgive their worst enemies?"

"Well—Michael never said anything about that to me that I bring to mind. We are ordered, I know, not to hate any one, an' we are to pray for our enemies. The prayer is often said backwards, I'm afraid. But why we'd dislike a body because we do him a harm, is a brain-puzzler to me."

"Yet, it is so, Mary. We know that those we injure will be revengeful towards us."

"And why not?—barring they are good Christians entirely, entirely?"

"And, because we know they will be resentful towards us, we fear them: we regard them as our enemies, and dislike them as such."

"Ah, then!—may-be so."

"There is another cause, Mary, why we dislike those we have injured."

"I see I didn't mistake when I said you had the schooling an' the worldly craft. I'd like to know the other cause, Sir, if you haven't any objection."

"When we see the person we have injured, or when we reflect on the wrong we have done him, conscience stings us painfully, and the sting is the more intolerable, the greater the injury we have inflicted———."

"Well, well, well!—let me ponder awhile. Supposing that you're a landlord, an' that you take the land from a poor creature that has nothing else to get his living from, an' that you turn him out of house an' land, an' send him poor and penniless on the world, himself, an' his wife, an' his flock of childre:—you think he won't forget it to you, an' you don't like a bone in his skin."

"Precisely so, Mary;—you have my meaning."

I have truthfully given the ethical analysis wrought out between Mary Hanrahan and myself; and I will here forestall the reader's smile at my expense by acknowledging that I was urged by my vanity to prove to Mary that I was able to "unriddle" her riddle. I wished to justify to her her flattering appreciation of my "worldly craft an' schooling." I thought I had gained my point, and was self-complacent thereon.

"And now, Mary," I continued, laying my finger on her shoulder, "I will show you how it is that our reasoning bears on the question you have asked me. You seek to know why it was that your 'victim of intemperance,'—you seem to approve of the term?"—

"It fits him like a glove."

"Why your victim of intemperance was more harsh to those he had loved than to strangers.

"Your victim of intemperance was obliged to acknowledge to himself that he had injured and outraged his pure and affectionate wife; that in return for her love and devotion, he had repaid her by slight, perhaps by falsehood even. When her wasted form, and her pale, terrified face met his eye, conscience whispered to him—with a whisper louder in his ear than the thunder-clap—that the withering of her beauty, and the shattering of her health was his work. And, Mary, he could shout and sing with the decayed gentleman, because he had done *him* no injury; and he was harsh and cruel towards his wife because he could not close his ears against the cries of conscience. Do I make myself understood, Mary?" I asked, with the impressive manner of a lecturer.

"Ah, then! indeed I can't say, Sir, that I undherstand you all out entirely. But no blame—you know I haven't the craft or the schooling."

There was a sly undervaluing of my doctrine in the backward motion of Mary's head, and in her look, that humbled my self-complacency considerably.

"I don't say but your words may be right enough.

But I'll tell you my notion: it isn't mine all out, but Michael's. I think that the grace of God never shields the dhrinking man, an' that he falls entirely into the power of the worker of all evil. May heaven guard us from temptation!" she reverently added, forming the sign of the cross with her thumb on forehead, lips, and breast.

"Well, Mary, yours may be the shortest and best explanation, after all," I said, modestly.

"Indeed, I think so, myself. 'Tis the plainest to me, at any rate."

There was a pause in our conference.

"Mary, were the Colonel and Richard O'Meara reconciled to each other?"

"They never were, Sir. Michael was forced to beg an' pray of the Curnel to keep out of the victim's way, an' not to come to our place any more. Michael and myself had the dhread on us they'd fly at aich other like game-cocks. The Curnel was hot an' peppery, as we had good reason to know; an' that the victim wouldn't take another whacking without paying the score back again 'twas aisy to foretell. The Curnel wasn't a bit cute—what good did *our* cuteness do us, I wondher? The Curnel had no skill in laying plans;—if we weren't such planners, poor Michael an' myself, maybe we'd be better off. But we turned the Curnel into a chip in porridge—neither harm nor good, poor man."

"And did the Colonel keep his resolution of total abstinence from liquor?"

"He never let a dhrop of anything sthronger than tay cross his lips as long as he stopped among us.

"Well, well," said Mary, after she had in silence gazed down for a while at the billows that broke in white foam against the little beach beneath our "cobbey house" in the cliff—

"Well, well, 'tis a comfort to bring to mind the times we had before our grief came on us. The Curnel was the apple of our eye to us. Every day that he got up, he paid us a visit. There was our poor dog Teague that's no more—may—I was going to say,—'may his soul rest in peace,' only I bethought of myself in time. We knew by Teague always when the Curnel was coming. Teague would hear the punch, punch, of the Curnel's leg—ay, I'm sure two miles away. Supposing that he was taking his doze on the hall-mat, or outside the door in the sun, he'd rouse himself up with a jump an' he'd cock his ears, an' he'd listen.

"'Teague snuffs the Curnel, maybe,' Michael would say. An' sure enough, the poor dog would throt down the garden-walk to the gate;—an' he'd stand on his hind legs, an' he'd rise the latch, an' he'd go down the road an' he'd wait there, wagging his tail. An' in six or seven minutes or so, the Curnel would be seen forcing his way on. An' my poor Teague would trot off to meet him. The Curnel tutored the dog to shake hands with him every day. He'd say 'Paw!' to Teague, an' my poor Teague would sit himself down, an' he'd laugh up in the Curnel's face—ay, as plain as you could laugh yourself, if you were in humour for it. An' you never saw the gentleman that would sthretch out his hand in a nater manner;—this way—"

And Mary, giving her right hand a twirl extended it towards me.

"This way he'd give out his paw, and the Curnel would shake hands with him most heartily, to be sure. I'm not telling you one word of untruth—my own eyes saw the meeting between them as often as I have fingers and toes—ay, indeed,—oftener by far.

"Well, Sir, Teague an' the Curnel would march up together to the cottage. The Curnel would make a grand salute to our darling, an' say, 'Maw—Ma-dame!' An' then he'd stare at her for half-an-hour or more, without opening his mouth again, till she'd grow fidgety. He'd toss up the baby, an' the baby would crow for him,—an' our young Dicky he'd sit riding on his leg. And all the time you'd say he was a cross-grained looking man. But the childre an' Teague an' all of us took delight in him. After a while he'd take Dicky by the hand; an' Teague, an' Dicky, an' the Curnel would march off together. Either Michael or myself—often Michael an' myself—glad of the excuse, you know, would follow afther them, side-by-side. The Curnel, if you please, had thrained Masther Dicky to fire off his leg. It would amuse you, indeed, if you were to see the brave little boy and the Curnel together. You never saw a pair on a cleverer understanding together than our manly, bowld Dicky an' the Curnel. 'Tis often I saw the Curnel winking his left eye at Dicky till you'd think he'd glue it together never to open it again. As sure as the wink was winked, an' that was every fine day, Dicky would take patthern by his teacher, an' wink as hard as the Curnel himself. An' then away they'd go on their walk, with Teague at their heels, or trotting on before them. I towld you, I think, that the Curnel had thrained our Dicky to shoot off his leg. The Curnel would stick out his leg, this way—"

Mary fixed her own leg on a rock directly opposite to her as she sat, that I might have ocular evidence of the Colonel's plan of proceeding.

—"An' Teague would sit down with a phiz as serious as if he was going to preach a sermon.

"Then you'd see Dicky, every joint in his body alive, stuffing the powdher into the leg. An' then he'd jump up an' sit straddle-legs on it, an' he'd set it going. An' the smoke an' the fire would come out of it surprising to see, an' if you were within hearing the noise would frighten you. But my stout little Dicky would keep firm in his saddle, an' at every shot that came from the leg he'd shout like a fellow in a scrimmage at a fair. An' Teague would bark, bark, until you'd think he'd lose his wits.

"Tis often and often I clapped my hands and laughed my 'nough at their sport. An' while the boy shouted, an' Teague barked, barked, barked,—you'd see the Curnel slapping the child on the back an' shaking hands with Teague, in as high glee as either the boy or the dog, only he'd have the cross-grained face all the time."

"What you have just described to me, Mary, refers to the time when Richard O'Meara and the Colonel were on friendly terms?"

"Oh, yes;—yes, indeed."

"The intimacy at the cottage did not, I suppose, continue after the quarrel on the bridge?"

"No, it did not. Michael, you know, had to beg of the Curnel not to come there. But for all that, often an' often, we'd hear a whistle that would pierce your ears. An' whenever the whistle was heard, nothing could keep Teague or Dicky at home, an' to a certainty they'd meet the Curnel down by the water-side. There's a brook running into the river not far off, an' 'tis through a glen the brook runs. An' in the glen Teague an' Dicky would find the Curnel, an' there they'd have their sports together. But the poor Curnel never came to the cottage again after the whacking on the bridge."

CHAPTER XXXV.

RICHARD O'MEARA'S PLEASANT, HEARTY LETTER TO HIS ELLEN.

I HAVE not, as I before intimated, followed the infatuated Richard O'Meara during his reckless career of intemperance. I will allow three years to pass over before I again take up the course of my narrative.

During that period Richard O'Meara had continued, with scarcely an interruption, to drink, drink constantly, until he had reached the final stage of his calamity—until he had reached that stage at which drunkards invariably arrive. He had reached that condition of physical and mental debility when even for the shortest space of time, existence is unendurable, unless the excitement produced by intoxicating liquor imparts an insane vivacity to the eye, a thriftless volubility to the tongue, a temporary tension and energy to the quivering nerves and muscles. The opium-eater must have his drug, and the tippler must have his drink, or the opium-eater and the tippler will both cringe from themselves and collapse into inanity. To this factitious state of being the continued use of inebriating liquor surely leads.

I shall not pause to analyze the physica causes producing this result, although direct physical causes could be assigned for it. If this final condition of the drunkard creates aversion, and merits condemnation, it is calculated at the same time to arouse our pity and commiseration.

Professional business, Richard O'Meara averred, required his presence in Dublin. This was a falsehood. For some time he had had no professional engagements whatever; no one had sought his professional services. Not one of his own family; not one of the inquisitors of "The Town of the Cascades" believed him when he asserted that the success of an important law-suit depended on his personal supervision. There was a time when Richard O'Meara would not have spoken falsely. Alas! the slave to intemperance loses caste, morally, socially, physically.

To Dublin Richard O'Meara journeyed, however, professedly to attend the courts. He was absent beyond a month. During that time he had written home but once; the third day after his departure the letter was received. It was placed in my hands by Michael Hanrahan, and I copy it here. It was apparently written while the pen was held in the fingers of one under the influence of the illusive and temporary glare which habitual tipplers mistake for sunshine. There was something like a momentary glimpse of right feeling, but miserably erratic. Evidently it was not written to give pain. Yet the already cicatrized heart of the reader received from it another gash; its perusal gave an addition to the heavy load of grief that already weighed her down.

Dublin, October 12th, 18—.

"My very dearest Ellen,

"Here I am, safe and sound, without a scratch or a scrape, sound wind and limb, and hearty as a buck, although I can't jump so high.

"My spirits were down below zero when I left home—all affectionate husbands like myself are so, or ought to be so, when by important business they are obliged to leave the charge of the nest entirely to their mate. There was about me a crankiness foreign to my nature, a peevishness that irritated me against myself, and put me in a humour to quarrel with every one or any one, if I could only get the colour of a pretext. I actually felt an itching to quarrel with myself first, and then to pummel all within reach of my arm, right and left, old and young, male and female, without regard to sex or age. By the highest of luck, however, I found myself in company with three of the best-natured fellows I ever met.

"We helped ourselves to a 'drop of the creature' wherever a drop was to be got. And fun and frolic, wit and waggery, jest and jocularity, lush and laughter (this alliteration is spontaneous, be sure of it), was the rule of the road all along to the end of the journey—"

When Ellen O'Meara had read thus far, she covered her pale, cold face with the letter. For a long, long time, no smile had lighted her husband's face for her. His manner had been, to speak moderately, cold and unkind. For the most part he had behaved, whenever at home, harshly, often violently. And Ellen, while her heart pined for his company, had feared to meet him,—had tremblingly sought to avoid him.

Alas! alas! She had learned to understand but too distinctly how it was that when away from her he could be the leader of mirth, and the loudest laugher. She understood but too well that to him she was no pleasant, boozing companion, but a neglected wife.

Ellen O'Meara inquired of her heart, while she held the letter against her face, was it not cruel of her Richard thus to describe to her his immoderate enjoyment with chance companions, while to her he was so cold and repulsive? Keen was the pang of that heart in reply to her query; and painful was its throb as she admitted to herself that the levity of the writer was produced by his besetting sin. She was obliged again and again to wipe her eyes before she could read on. I resume the letter.

"Ellen, now mind me, you little pussy, don't be jealous of what I have to tell you. For a good distance of my way I was next neighbour to one of the finest, dashingest, merriest girls in the world. Not to be compared with you, however, my old woman, when you were in your prime. No—I will say that for you.

"As a matter of course, you know, I was a most impressible, most bewitched bachelor, at her service. Not the slightest suspicion on her part that I had left a wife and three children at home to lay claim to me—"

Ellen O'Meara uttered a cry of agony. The

tears gushed plenteously from her eyes, and pattered on the paper.

"Oh, oh!" she sobbed out, "we have *not* three children. Oh! heartless father, two of our darlings are with their God. Oh! Richard, you their father, do you forget that we have lost them? or has their loss so little affected you that you make a jest of it to their mother? And, Richard, Richard,—you—"

She curbed herself, and she shuddered from head to foot as she did so, and her face assumed an expression of painful terror. The love she bore her husband had been so deeply impressed on her plastic nature that nothing short of death could efface it. The accusation her wounded mind had partly shaped was incompatible with the love she clung to, and shudderingly she cast it from her. No—her Richard had *not* been the cause of her children's death. It had been—the will of God!

"Oh, dearest Richard," she moaned, "why will you try me so? Why, why, will you tax my love so exigeantly?"

The letter went on thus:—

"I have in the inside of my pocket-book, together with one of her 'follow me quick' ringlets, the address of this charming creature. She has a fine dower in lands and ready cash, and by the soul in my body, if 'twere allowable under the Christian dispensation, I would prosecute my suit. Unhappily, polygamy is an indictable offence. In this land of so-called liberty, our freedom of action is no freedom at all, and I needs must bound my views to one wife—and one only. I positively think of giving up my faith in the gospel, and swearing by the Turkish Koran.

"But until I do, I subscribe myself, my dearest Ellen,

"Your 'Paddy Cary' of a husband,

"RICHARD O'MEARA."

The whole of the day on which this playful letter was received, Ellen O'Meara held it bitterly in her hand, and wept over it. And days and days were so spent by her.

It was, as I have said, the only letter she received

during her husband's absence. It was dated from Dublin only, so Ellen could not reply to it. But in truth she felt no disposition to write. How could she have shaped a reply to that cruel letter? Even in the need for counsel and protection that shortly came upon her, she knew not where to find her husband.

CHAPTER XXXVI.

WHAT MICHAEL HANRAHAN'S GAY MASK COVERED.

NEARLY six weeks passed before Richard O'Meara made his appearance again in his cottage.

During this time, the uneasiness of Michael Hanrahan's mind was tantalizing to him. The melancholy conviction forced itself on him that suspense and sorrow were rapidly working with fatal effect on "his angel," as he continued to name her. So that on her account and on his own he was urged to visit the town twice or thrice daily to question carriers of goods, drivers of public vehicles, and any travellers he could light on.

But from none could he obtain intelligence of his foster-brother. Mary and he had, as usual, consulted together on the necessity for these visits.

Mary never on any occasion differed from Michael, and she was convinced that the inquiries should be prosecuted diligently.

The work of necessity was to be carried on cautiously, however. If Michael were to make manifest the great anxiety that preyed on him, ill-natured and injurious conclusions would be arrived at by the eager gossipers of the town. After mature deliberation, a plan was devised between "the pair of Solomons," calculated to blink the widow-woman and all such news-carriers.

Michael shrewdly judged that there was an espionage at the post-office to detect the arrival of letters. And he was not mistaken in his conjecture. For really, the mysterious absence of Richard O'Meara was to be accounted for to the satisfaction of the town, *coûte que coûte*. It was known that one letter only had passed through "the post," and Michael would cunningly give it to be understood that every day, and often twice in the day, letters had been received; but that for substantial reasons of his own "Masther Dick" had sent them by hand.

The constant inquiries of Michael were to be for letters, and while on the perquisition for them he could put other questions, carelessly to all appearance, but most astutely directed, for all that.

To carry out the "plan" in the most effectual manner, Michael was to assume a gay-fellow demeanour, "not to seem down in the mouth at all;" and he was to make believe as if nothing in the world troubled him. If any inquisitive people, Toby Purcell for instance, were to put plump questions to him about home, Michael was to aver that the angel was in blooming health, and as gay as a linnet of a summer's morning. But for fear her poor white face might be noticed, even through the thick folds of her veil, when she was able to creep to the chapel, he might give a hint that she was likely to be laid up soon in a certain way. But he must not go far on that head.

Poor Michael! many a bitter struggle it cost him to mould his flexible features into an assumption of gaiety, while sadness gnawed his heart. And after all, it was duplicity to no purpose. Mary told me how Michael and herself subsequently discovered that no one was deceived, and that notwithstanding all his cleverness, Michael was laughed at, almost to his face, by "Toby Purcell an' the rest of them;" ay, even when he thought he had been most successful.

There was one person, however, to meet whom Michael had no necessity to wear his mask. And surely was it beyond measure a relief to Michael to escape, as he expressed it, "from calling it a summer's day when the black frost of grief was in the very marrow of his bones." And it was with one of those long-drawn sighs that escape us when we are relieved from great pain, that Michael would turn to the bridge after having made his fruitless inquiries, to look out for the Half-pay.

It is a sheerly selfish instinct that impels us to seek a confidant in our troubles. We are urged by an innate conviction that we will lighten the load we carry, for a time, at least, when we can find one for whose inspection we can unpack our burthen.

When, shoulder to shoulder, the Half-pay and Michael leaned over the bridge together, and that

Michael had, as it were, flung his town-mask into the river below, it was like a generous balsam to his feelings to reveal the real state of affairs at the cottage to one who loved and pitied the angel, as sincerely and as heartily as himself. And to one, moreover, who did not controvert Michael's doctrine that his foster-brother was one of the most lovable of men "only for the cursed dhrink;" in fact that the drink was entirely to blame for existing evils, and not the drinker,—Richard O'Meara, owing to its vile power, not being an accountable person.

It was during one of these unburthening, confidential interviews between Michael and the Half-pay, that Michael related, in a low, sad voice, which often failed him as he went on, that the bloom of the rose was gone entirely entirely from the angel's cheeks, and that she had the look of a living corpse. Her lips even, that had been of such a "shiney" red, appearing like wetted paper, they were so white and moist. And Michael informed his sympathizing listener that the angel was wasted away to a skeleton, and that she coughed "a churchyard cough." That some days she was unable to rise from her bed, and that a walk from one room to another, even with Mary's tender help, was a wearisome journey to her.

Was it not, think you, an emancipation that Michael Hanrahan longed for, to doff his fool's cap with its jangling bells, to rub away the paint, to discard the grimace, and shoulder to shoulder with his eccentric friend, whisper the sad reality into the ear of so sincere a sharer of his sorrow? And were not the abrupt, but to Michael expressive, ejaculations of the Half-pay consoling to him?

Yes, indeed. This fellowship was eagerly sought for by Michael, and ardently offered by the Half-pay.

Day after day passed, and Michael Hanrahan had still no more cheering report to make. The angel spent her days and her nights listening for the sound of her husband's voice, and then crying over the hope deferred. And instead of her husband's voice, the bold tones of Nora Spruhan's, in loud contention with Michael, often met her ear, and terrified and shocked her.

The Half-pay, by two short words, "Thrash—her!" and by an explanatory action with his cudgel, proposed a remedy for this latter grievance, and was even starting off to carry his threat into effect. But Michael, foreseeing the consequences, dissuaded him from trying the unpromising experiment.

A few days further on, and Michael had even more painful intelligence to communicate.

There was no money in the cottage, there was no food beyond a scanty stock of potatoes, the vegetables of the garden, and the milk of the cows. These were good enough for Mary and himself, and they gave God thanks for them and used them. But there was Nora Spruhan—she clamoured against such diet, and filled the house with her brawling. And there was the angel. The angel must perish without a little wine, and something tempting in the way of solid food. It was little, very little sufficed for her, but it should be good and nourishing. After casting his eyes cautiously round to ascertain that no strangers witnessed his proceeding, Michael exhibited to the Half-pay some articles of plate he had brought with him to dispose of. But Michael was sadly perplexed where to find a market. Michael did not at all regard what people might say of himself. It would chime in with his views even if they should judge harshly of him, and say that he was plundering his foster-brother in his absence. If people would only think in this way, Michael wouldn't mind. The Lord would see him and understand him, and he was satisfied. But then, if he offered the articles for sale here and there, an exposure of the destitution and misery at the cottage might follow. The predicament was a stumbling-block to Michael.

To be sure he could go to the county town, and in this way avoid exposure. But what was to happen while he was away? Who could answer for the dreaded Nora Spruhan?

"Stop—here!"

And the Half-pay stumped off in the direction of his little house above the river with the alertness—if not the grace—of a boy. In a very short time Michael saw him descend, as briskly as the nature of the ground would permit, and they were again leaning over the bridge, shoulder to shoulder.

The Half-pay seized Michael's hand, by no means gently. He placed a soft substance within that hand, and squeezed the fingers so tightly against the palm that Michael involuntarily winced from the force of the pressure. When the gripe was relaxed, Michael Hanrahan opened his fingers and examined his palm. There was more than one bank-note there. He looked at his friend with tears of gratitude overflowing his eyes.

"May the Lord give you his grace and blessing!" was ejaculated in a broken voice. And the Half-pay returned Michael's look so fixedly and sternly that a passing observer might have imagined he glanced defiance and resentment from beneath his knotted brows.

A few days farther on, and Michael Hanrahan had no need to appear in the "Town of the Cascades" with his mask of levity on. Further ill-acted disguise was unnecessary. It could not be kept secret that the sheriff of the county had, in technical parlance, "laid an execution" there, and that his officers were in charge. It could not be concealed from the widow-woman, or from "Toby Purcell and the rest of them," that an auction of all that was saleable, including the cow that gave the milk, and the small stock of potatoes, was to take place in a few days.

Most abjectly, but vainly, did Michael Hanrahan entreat of the bailiff employed taking an inventory of the effects, not to force his way into the bed-room of his sick angel. By a bribe, part of the Half-pay's gift, a compromise was effected, and a delay granted. And the panting, shivering Ellen sat as a looker-on while the bailiff, aided by his companion who held the "ink-horn," added to his inventory the furniture of the apartment, even to the bed from which she had just risen.

The legal time for "the sheriff's sale" came on, and for the greater part of two days the Cottage of the Cascades was in possession of a crowd, every one that wished entering without a question, and hurrying from room to room. The house was in an uproar; there was rushing and tramping; there were jests and laughter; there was the loud din of many voices. And at length everything was bought up and taken away, and the pleasant Cottage of the Cascades was bare and silent,—bare and silent, with one exception.

The bed-room of the angel, and the sitting-room adjoining, had not not been despoiled. The Half-pay had outbid all competitors for the furniture of these two rooms, so they remained intact.

To a certain extent the privacy of the suffering "angel" had been preserved through all the clamour of the sheriff's sale. The Half-pay and Michael Hanrahan had stood as sentinels at her door.

The Half-pay's look of prohibition, and Michael Hanrahan's pleading words prevented intrusion to a great degree. So that Ellen was but little gazed at as she sat within her chamber listening to the turmoil without, with what fortitude she could command.

And yet, while poverty and wreck came on the once pleasant home, there were no tidings of the absent Richard O'Meara.

CHAPTER XXXVII.

RICHARD O'MEARA'S RETURN.

WHEN a week had passed over, and that Michael Hanrahan, notwithstanding his unrivalled tact and diligence, had failed to gain intelligence of his truant foster-brother, he made it a point not to permit an evening to go by without joining the assemblage of beggars and livers on chance at the widow-woman's door, where the public car, conveying passengers in the direction to and from the metropolis, drew up.

For many weary evenings did he return thence to the cottage with trailing step, drooping and downcast. At length, on the tenth evening subsequent to the sheriff's sale, the watchful Michael recognized the voice of the person he looked for, even while the car was driving down the main street towards his stand.

He recognized the voice before he could visibly distinguish his foster-brother, for it was loud and mirthful. Humour and frolic were going on amongst the passengers, and the voice and laugh of Richard O'Meara were recognizable by Michael above those of the other participators in the glee.

Michael Hanrahan's assumption of gaiety had been cast aside since the distress at the cottage had been made public, and as he leaned against the jamb of the widow-woman's door, any one could tell that he was woe-begone and desponding.

When the car pulled up, and that he saw Richard O'Meara spring down buoyantly, and accost his fellow-passengers and the lookers-on with exuberant jollity of manner, the "welcome home," stuck in his throat, and he could not give it utterance.

Michael did not fail to remark the effect produced on the observers by Richard O'Meara's conduct.

The beggars, clamorous towards others, did not accost him: none of their voluble prayers, so profusely showered on every one else, were uttered for him: they whispered together, and, as Michael feared, they muttered curses against him. Not one of the eager candidates for chance-employment offered service to him. If a neighbour passed, the boisterously-jovial Richard O'Meara was regarded with aversion, and was avoided. All this Michael saw and felt as keenly as if he were himself the one publicly condemned as the exhibitor of unnatural levity, while poverty and approaching death were in his ruined home.

The mastiff, Teague, had accompanied Michael on his look-out. He had started off to meet the car, and came gambolling by its side as it approached. His whine of recognition and welcome was acknowledged by his master, and his demonstrations of affection were cordially returned. Michael, too, was recognized, and his foster-brother shook him gaily by both hands.

"Michael, my boy," Richard O'Meara cried out

aloud; "ha!—you're here, by Jove! to meet me. Rejoiced I am to find you so hale and stout; a sample of good living, and of pleasant days, and sound sleep of nights."

The speaker stooped and whispered in Michael's ear.

"Hie you home, Michael," he said, "and tell the mistress I shall be with her shortly. And, Michael, my worthy, mind that you have a savoury, delicious supper for us. We shall celebrate my return happily and lovingly, your mistress and I—that we will, by Jove! Hie you off now, Michael, and announce my arrival, in prime order, as you see."

Richard O'Meara did not keep his engagement with Michael. He did not spend the evening with his wife. During many hours of darkness she had watched for him, and he came not. At length his footsteps resounding along the garden walk were heard through the stillness of the night. He was admitted by Michael. Even then his wife hoped he would seek her, but he did not. Without speaking, he entered the room nearest at hand. There he sank on the floor, and was very soon in a profound but uneasy slumber.

And his Ellen?

She stole into the denuded room where her husband lay. She sat down on the floor close to him, she placed his head upon her lap, and there cradled it. She passed her thin white hand across his forehead and through his hair; with the touch of her chilly fingers she cooled his heated brow. And so she sat during the continuance of darkness, propped up after a while by the arms of Mary, who had come in search of her. And Ellen O'Meara sat there when the November morning looked in upon her coldly and uncheeringly.

About two hours after the leaden dawn stole in, Richard O'Meara awoke from his feverish sleep. He looked upwards. His wife's gentle, unreproaching eyes met his. After a momentary pause he sprang to his feet; he gazed confusedly at the watcher of the night, as with hands pressed together she sat looking upwards into his face. There was terror and bewilderment in his rolling eyes and quivering features and heaving chest. He clasped his head between both his hands with a strong pressure, and looked round, and round, and downward.

"Ellen, Ellen," he at length gasped out, "where am I? What do you do sitting there so wan and ghost-like? Injured, wronged, and ill-requited Ellen, rise up from that lowly position. Rise from that prostration, Ellen! Save me from interminable despair by bringing back the colour to your sunken cheeks; and let the glowing blood glisten through the film of your lips again; and oh! let not the sweet blue of your eyes retreat from me so."

Deeply agitated, he knelt, and cast his arms around her, and raised her up, and held her in his embrace.

"I have been ill—very ill, Richard, during your absence," she gently said.

"That is but too visible to me, Ellen. Ha! you are dying—dying in my very arms! There is no pulsation in her heart, and her eyes are closed,—and her limbs that were so elastic trail helplessly—"

As he spoke what his distracted mind suggested, his gaze wandered round and round the apartment.

"How—how is this?" he cried. "Surely this is our drawing-room. Where is the furniture? Where is the sofa on which I might lay my Ellen?"

"In the parlour, Richard," Ellen faintly answered. "In the parlour I can lie down."

"Oh, oh!" he groaned, "I had forgotten—now it recurs to me—that some one—somewhere—told me of this. I forget where I was told it, or who told it—I spurned him from me; I now see it was no falsehood to tell me that my home was stripped to the bare walls, and that my wife's tender limbs had no softer resting-place than the naked boards."

"Help me to the parlour, dear Richard," petitioned the exhausted Ellen.

He raised her in his strong arms, and bore her into the parlour. He laid her gently on the sofa, and settled the cushions under her head. There was wine on the sideboard; he poured some into a glass, and held it to her lips. She swallowed it eagerly, and before long gained strength to raise herself to a sitting posture.

Richard O'Meara, his hands pressed forcibly against his temples, walked round, and round, and round the room. For some minutes the rapid circuit was continued. He paused, drew a chair slowly towards him, seated himself opposite his wife, and addressed her.

"Ellen,—my guilt might not be so appallingly hideous to me had I met you in robust health, angrily casting your reproaches on me, and accusing me of the wrongs I have heaped on you. But oh!—to find you passing away so lamb-like to your death, without one word of reproach from your lips, convicts me to myself of being the most detestable scoundrel that exists,—even I who sit here gazing on the ruin of your beauty."

"Dear Richard, let us look forward with hope in the goodness of God. You will leave me no more, and we shall yet be happy together—ay, even as happy as we used to be."

"More abundant blessings could not be granted mortal than were bestowed on me," Richard O'Meara said, following up the train of thought presented to his distracted brain while he had hurried round the room—"I possessed superabundant health, and I had the energy that health bestows. I had the power, and the capacity, and the opportunity, to win my way honourably to wealth and distinction. The Creator of the good and beautiful granted to me the love of one of the most perfect of his creatures. This sweet being, with open hand and open heart, trustingly blessed me with herself—gave to my keeping her wealth. I have cast all these favours from me. I have flung away health, energy, industry, character! In return for my wife's innocent love and uncalculating trust, I have dragged her down with me to unmitigated destitution and pauperism, and have hurried her from the heyday of her young life to an untimely grave!"

"Richard, my own dear Richard, be moderate in your self-accusation. I shall recover, with heaven's help—"

"To beggary and want!"

"Surely, dearest husband, we shall not be destitute? There will be sufficient in what remains to us. There is the settlement you insisted on making at our marriage. That is not trifling, and with peace and love, we shall be rich enough."

"Destitute—utterly, totally destitute, Ellen,—you have yet to learn the full extent of your destroyer's villainy. Your settlement is gone—gone—squandered at the gaming-table. From the bottom of my foul heart do I hope you will take the only step that can recover your property."

"For your sake, and for our child's, dearest Richard, I will do whatever you advise."

"Then listen to me, Ellen. You must prosecute your dastardly betrayer for forgery. I forged your signature to the deed of conveyance. I am a felon. Convict me of the offence—it will be a mercy to me. Convicted of felony at the bar of justice, as I shall be, the deed of sale will be void. It will be a mercy to me."

Ellen covered her eyes, shuddered, and fell back insensible.

"Oh, God!" shouted Richard O'Meara, standing over her; "oh God of retributive justice, what punishment do I not deserve at your hands? God of justice, God of retribution, pour the full venom of your wrath upon my guilty head! Thy vengeance is my due."

CHAPTER XXXVIII.

THE WIFE'S GRAVE.

It was late in November when Richard O'Meara returned from his calamitous visit to Dublin.

It was now the eve of the Christmas-day following. In the Cottage of the Cascades no Christmas banquet was in preparation: no Christmas revelry was to go forward. Silent death, not laughing revelry, was the household ruler at the cottage. The eve of the Christmas-day succeeding the interview between her and her husband, as related in the last Chapter, Ellen O'Meara's funeral was to take place.

The month of December had rushed forward hand-in-hand with scowling, furious winter. All through, the weather had been severe even for the season, and Ellen's death had been accelerated by the rude contact. For some days and nights a biting frost had cleared the air, and the sun had shown through a chill, cloudless atmosphere, brightly and brilliantly, while at night, the most distant stars were visible, and sparkled cheerily. On the eve of the Christmas-day the blue of the sky was hidden by a dull, uniform leaden veil, and at the hour of three in the afternoon, when the coffin enclosing the remains of Ellen O'Meara was borne out of the cottage for burial, there was no view of the firmament, the snow fell so thickly.

In Ireland, funerals are not "performed,"—the term, I believe, used elsewhere. The expression of respect towards the deceased is not so much denoted by the display of the paraphernalia of mourning, as by the number of persons congregated to follow the remains.

Notwithstanding the severity of the weather, scarcely one of the inhabitants of our "Town of the Cascades" was absent from Ellen O'Meara's burial. The assemblage was increased by the attendance of the people from the surrounding country, so that when, according to custom, the coffin was placed on chairs outside the house of mourning, while prayers were offered for a happy eternity to the departed soul, the snow fell upon the uncovered heads of a dense crowd.

The body was not placed in a hearse, decorated with nodding plumes. Such a conveyance was not in the town. It was borne to the grave on the shoulders of those who volunteered their services. It is a notable proof of public estimation when the bearers of a coffin are frequently changed. It often occurs that the same supporters will walk but a pace or two under their burthen, when they are replaced by others.

This evidence of respect and esteem was eagerly displayed at Ellen O'Meara's funeral. And so constant had been the pauses, while the removal from shoulder to shoulder was being effected, that the progress made was very slow. By the time the procession had clambered to the hill-top churchyard described at the opening of this narrative, the short, gloomy day was closing in, and the feathery insignia of winter's reign was coming down thicker and thicker, as if in representation of a chilly winding-sheet.

Richard O'Meara walked close behind his wife's coffin, and his boy walked beside him. Mere children are but momentarily affected by the sight of death. For the most part the novelty of the attendant circumstances impresses them more forcibly than the incident itself. Richard O'Meara's son was now, however, in his thirteenth year. He felt the nature of his bereavement with all a boy's fresh ardour, and he wept and sobbed aloud without curb or disguise.

Richard O'Meara's head drooped forward, as lowly as it could fall; it was supported by his chin resting against his chest. He glanced not to the right or left; he sought no sympathy; he looked into no eye to ask commiseration; he claimed no word of solace.

Had Richard O'Meara craved compassion throughout the crowd of which he was the centre, none would have been accorded him. It was the general credence that the premature death of his wife was the direct result of personal violence. And it was whispered from one to the other, that it would have been more seemly had he been absent on the present occasion, than to walk with the tottering gait of inebriation, behind her corpse. Richard O'Meara, had he sought commiseration, would have met reproach and blame.

"There wasn't a Christian crature there, young or old, gentle or simple, that had a feeling for him —not one!" were Michael Hanrahan's words. "The poor, heart-sore fellow. Heaven above knows, an', mind you, I'm right certain my words are truth,—he'd stretch himself in the one grave with the angel at the same moment, if he could;— an' he'd cry out to them to shovel the churchyard clay fast over him, to hide him from all eyes but the One—the eye that nothing can be hidden from. Ay, indeed, he would."

Michael looked upward, and crossed his forehead.

"Ah!" he sighed, "the neighbours were too sorely heavy on him. Maybe, if the honest truth was told, there was many a one among them that lived in glass houses themselves. Many a one of them, maybe, oughtn't to throw stones at their neighbours. 'Tisn't the best Christian that finds out the faults of others the soonest.

"Ah!" sighed Michael again, "the Lord be good to us all."

After a thoughtful pause, he continued:

"Myself and the good, honest dog, Teague, walked at the funeral, just behind of the fosther-brother an' young Dicky. I could hear, as plain as you hear me now, what was said among the people. An' if *he* wasn't as deaf as a milestone, he heard what was said too. But he didn't heed it. They couldn't say worse of him than he thought about himself, poor fellow."

At the entrance to the elevated cemetery wherein the grave had been already prepared, the body, in conformity with the universal custom amongst Catholics in Ireland, was lowered from the shoulders of the men who had borne it so far. Six fresh volunteer assistants stepped out eagerly from the crowd. They clasped their hands together in pairs, and on the arms thus linked, the coffin was deposited. The attendant clergyman, his hat raised, but held so as to protect his head in some degree from the snow, then walked slowly forward, reciting the burial service. With bared heads the funeral attendants followed, joining in the responses. In this order the remains were carried round the graveyard before being deposited on the edge of the excavation in which they were to be laid.

It may seem to my Irish readers that the notice of this ceremony, never dispensed with, is an intrusion here. A circumstance occurred, however, while the procession moved round the churchyard, which cannot be passed over, and which renders the allusion incidental.

As Richard O'Meara, with bare head exposed to the fast descending snow-flakes, walked close at the coffin-foot, he stumbled, and fell heavily. As he went down, his temple struck against a lowly head-stone; a deep gash was inflicted, and the blood gushed over his face and down his person.

Michael Hanrahan, the prostrate man's son, and the dog Teague, alone hurried to raise him up. He was momentarily stunned, and did not at once recover. Michael and the lad had not bodily strength to effect their purpose, and Michael piteously appealed for aid. Not one of the lookers-on offered a helping hand. The clergyman alone, when he understood the cause of interruption, hastened back and gave his assistance. The bleeding man quickly regained his strength, and the circuit of the churchyard was completed.

The coffin was placed in the grave; the stones and clay fell with a hollow sound upon it, and the little elevation marking the place of rest was shaped and sodded by the willing hands of the neighbours. There is a peculiar taste, if the term may be used, exemplified in the fashioning and trimming of a grave-mound, for which some humble funereal attendants possess a recognized talent. This taste was cheerfully exercised in moulding Ellen O'Meara's grave-mound.

While the coffin was descending into its repository,—while the stones and clay were thrown on it, and while the grave-mound was moulding and sodding,—Richard O'Meara, still bare-headed, leaned upon a head-stone that overlooked the spot. On the coffin-lid spots of blood fell from his temple: the workers below did not wipe them away. They left them red as they fell. The dripping blood mingled with the covering of clay and stones, and rained on the sodded elevation when it was shaped and trimmed.

The thick darkness of the winter-night had not as yet shrouded the hill-top churchyard, when the grave was perfected to the satisfaction of the neighbours, who had wrought at it with such kind will: but the murky screen was closing rapidly. The large funereal assemblage had nearly dispersed; a few only, in addition to those engaged as workers, had remained: these had tarried to the last, charitably intent on discharging what they considered a last duty to the dead.

The shovel and spade used in the work of burial were laid, in representation of a cross, on "the narrow house" just sealed up. The neighbours stood around in a circle, and uncovered their heads. Michael Hanrahan, as was known to those present, had been piously brought up; and he was tacitly acknowledged as the leader of the religious rite they were to join in.

The psalm "De Profundis" was recited, the verses repeated alternately by the leader and his respondents. The ceremony closed with a prayer for eternal happiness to the soul of the deceased. When this prayer had been prayed, shovel and pick and spade were shouldered, and "the pious neighbours," and the sealers-up of "the narrow house" descended with all necessary caution from the rocky hill-top churchyard to the town below.

But the hill-top churchyard was not left in the sole possession of the dead.

When the circle of "pious neighbours" had been formed for prayer, Richard O'Meara sank cautiously to his knees at the grave's foot. His voice was not heard, however, joining with the others.

"Maybe the poor fellow said to himself, 'I'm not worthy to offer up a prayer,'"—was Michael Hanrahan's interpretation of his silence.

When, after the concluding ritual, all the others had gone away, Michael Hanrahan, Richard O'Meara, Richard O'Meara's son, the dog Teague, and one other person remained.

Nearly an hour elapsed, and Richard O'Meara continued still kneeling at the grave's foot. The almost impenetrable darkness of night came on; and as it fell, the weather changed. It ceased to snow; the wind rose high, and heavy, drenching rain poured down. Yet Richard O'Meara, uncovered and bleeding, his head drooped upon his chest, as it had drooped at the funeral, knelt on the spot where he had first bent his knees.

"For the Lord's sake, come with us out of this!" Michael Hanrahan besought.

"Quit me, fiend of perdition! Be gone!"

Richard O'Meara shouted out this answer to Michael's solicitation so fiercely and so shrilly, that Michael recoiled from him. The still kneeling man raised his right arm very slowly, as if he were forcing it upwards. He laid the tips of his fingers against his forehead.

"In the name of the Father!"—he said, in a deep inward voice. He paused, and his arm fell as if paralyzed.

"He began the blessing of himself," observed Michael, addressing me with solemn earnestness of manner. "He began the blessing of himself;—he never finished it!

"From that moment to the present time that's in it, it was my thought, and it is my thought still, that if he had finished the blessing of himself,—'In the name of the Father, and of the Son, and of the Holy Ghost; Amen!'"—Michael suited the action to the word, crossing himself as Catholics do,—"the evil fate that was before him that night would not have come upon him. When he said, 'In the name of the Father,' he stopped, and he didn't say the other holy words! And then he gave a pitiful cry, an' he threw himself down the full length of his body along the new-made grave."

Michael Hanrahan was placed in a most difficult, —I would say, an alarming position. What was he to do with himself on such a dreary night, and in such a place? How was he to dispose of the drenched and shivering boy at his side? How was he to act towards the prostrate man who lay on his face along the grave?

Michael's own words will best describe the events that subsequently took place.

"Never before, and never since," he said, "was I out of such a night as that was. It was so out-an-out pitch dark, that when I stretched my hand from me to grope my way, the very hand belonging to my own body I couldn't see! The wind blew, up there on the top of the hill, so wicked that it put me on my best to keep my feet. Believe you me, that if you were blown down there, you'd be bruised to mummy among the tombstones and the headstones you couldn't see. Or maybe you'd be whipped, body and bones, down the hill that was of a sugarloaf shape at the side above the river. You know the churchyard yourself?"

"Yes, Michael; it was there I met your Mary; and in consequence of my visit on that occasion, you and she have from time to time made me acquainted with the story of Ellen O'Meara's grave."

"Just so,—sure enough," resumed Michael. "*I* never had the bad fortune, Lord be praised! to come across anything in the night-time worse than a Christian. But other people hadn't my luck. Often it came to pass that benighted men,—ay, and women as well as men,—met with the throubled spirits of the departed, in lonesome places, and in churchyards, and where blood was shed. If the sthrongest man that ever tossed a sledge, and the stoutest as well as the sthrongest, was to look on a throubled spirit, the sthrength or the courage wouldn't stay with him, and he'd faint dead, like a girl, the very moment he crossed a threshold and came among the living again."

"So I have heard, Michael."

"You may believe it for the truth. If you were in the churchyard where our angel—God rest her! —was buried; if you were there the night of her funeral, the darkness so heavy that you couldn't see an inch before you, and the rain an' the hail coming down as if the world was to be dhrowned a second time, and the roaring wind tearing here and there and everywhere,—my word for it but your heart would fail you."

"Certainly it was a dreary spot of such a night."

"Dreary, as you say, it was." And Michael cringed, and drew in his breath shudderingly at the recollection.

"If you were there as I was, you couldn't tell no more than myself if the moaning, an' the wailing, and the shouting that was among the tombs an' headstones, an' in the old church that stood among the graves, and down through the grove on the hill-side, came from the wind or from the throubled spirits of the dead people. Oh! that I may never be in such a place again of such a night as that, until the time comes when my eyes an' ears will be closed for ever, without the sight or hearing in them.

"As sure as I'm speaking to you, my teeth struck together so loud that myself was frightened at the noise they made, though I did my endeavours to keep them from making such a churchyard clatther.

"And there was my poor young Dicky. He crushed himself up against me as close as he could, an' I put my arms round his neck to make him understand he was not there alone. I could feel the shiver that was on him; I could feel every shake of his body; and sure it was no surprise that he should shiver and shake. He was soaked through to the skin as well as myself. If the terror was on me, that might be his father, it was no wondher the poor boy should shiver, from the wet, and cold, and fright."

"I am not surprised at it, Michael."

"It was a hard thrial to both of us to stop up there. Trying to think, the best I could, I remembered there was a friend not far away, and that friend was our good-hearted poor Curnel. Before the blinking light of the black evening went from us entirely, I saw the Curnel hobbling into the old church, an' I bethought me that he was there still. If ever one crature loved another, the Curnel loved our Dicky, and I thought within myself that I'd bring the perishing boy to the Curnel, an' who knows but he might coax him away out of the sleet an' darkness, an' the unnatural noises of the place. 'Hold me fast by the hand, Dicky,' I whispered to the child, as well as I could bring out the words. 'Hold me fast by the hand, an' come with me.'—'No, Michael,' he made answer, and I was obliged to bend down my ear to him to hear his words; 'you may go, Michael, if you are afraid to stay. You can go somewhere where there is light and people,' says he; 'go if you are afraid to stay. I will stop here to be company for my father and to take care of him. I'll stop here to help him up when he's done crying on my mother's grave.' Wasn't Dicky a brave, courageous boy, Sir?"

"A noble boy he was, Michael."

"I knew Dicky—no wondher that I should—I knew him to be headsthrong, and I knew that young as he was, the thing he'd say he'd do. He was a brave and a bould fellow for his years, an' I knew well, that if I couldn't dhrag him by main force over the graves an' the head-stones, he wouldn't leave the father there alone. I was sore afflicted, and like one losing his senses.

"'I'll go, in the Lord's name,' says I in my mind, 'an' I'll talk to the Curnel. If he *can* help us in our need, he *will* help us. If I can find my way to him, I'll bring him over near to us. He'll be company for us, an' this poor shaking boy and myself won't be all out so lonely an' so frightened when the Curnel is standing by. So, in heaven's name,'—and I made the sign of the cross on my forehead, as a bar betwixt me and the evil of the place,—'I'll try if I can feel my road through the pitch-dark.'

"I put out the two hands, as far as they could sthretch from me, an' I groped before me, an' to both sides of me, and I felt my way with one foot. And then I felt my way with the other foot, an' made a little step, and then I made another little step, and then another. There was a tall, black head-stone just before me: I could see it, for it was blacker than the night, black as that was. I laid my right hand this way on the black head-stone. I felt it moving undher the hand I laid on it."

"Michael, you were under the influence of great terror, and your shrinking imagination deceived you!"

"There was fear on me, no doubt, I won't deny it. You wouldn't get many to be free and easy and careless if they were in my place. But I tell you, as sure as that the same right hand is on your shouldher this present moment, so sure did the black head-stone move. And furthermore, as certain as that you see my mouth opening and shutting, and as certain as that you hear the words coming from my lips, the wrist of my right hand was grasped fast—fast as if there was an iron chain round it, and then the hand an' arm was dhragged from me the same as if a sthrong man was pulling at the chain with all his might."

"Michael?—Michael?"

"And," Michael continued, without pausing to notice my expression of dubious faith, "*words* were said to me. Not close up at my ear, but for all that, in through an' through the ear at the right side of my head the words came. You may give credit to me. The words were said in a whisper like a hiss, through an' through my right ear."

Michael paused as if to recollect himself, and then he went on speaking slowly, and with the impressiveness of one awed by his recollections.

"When 'tis a stormy night; when 'tis wild and wicked outside of a house; when the nails that fasten the hinges of the doors are started; when the bolts and latches are crookened by the blast forcing its way; and when the window-panes are dashed in about the floor;—though the noise of the storm within and without is enough to deafen you;—at the very same time you'll hear the angry wind screeching through the keyholes above an' below, wherever it finds a keyhole to screech through.

"The words that came through my ear were as plain to hear as the wind screeching through the keyhole in the storm. But the wind through the keyhole only screeches; it doesn't speak words, as that hissing, screeching whisper did. They were the words of a spirit of darkness and wickedness that I heard."

"What were the words you heard, Michael?"

"The words were said in the Irish speech. The Irish speech is plainer to the hearing, it goes to the heart more than the grandest of English does. I'll never, never forget the words screeched into my ear that pitch-dark, teeming, stormy night, up in the churchyard.

"I will say the words in the English for you. The evil spirit said in the Irish, '*He is mine—he is mine—he is mine!*' Three times it said that—'*mine and none to keep him from me,* MINE!' it said then. If you were there to hear them, they'd never quit your mind. They never will quit my mind. There was no sorrow in the voice that said them, they were screeched like as if the spirit they came from was glorifying afther a victory. You'd say 'twas a screech with gladness in it.

"You look at me as if you didn't give belief to me. But you *may* believe me. Although the marrow in my bones shivered, and although I could feel my blood creeping cold through me, until the heart within was frozen up, an' shrivelled to the size of a grain of corn like:—yet for all that, I had my hearing, an' I heard the evil words.

"I never said to any one, not to the priest himself, or to poor Mary, what I'm going to say to you now. I didn't like to say it because it might look like a sentence passed on my deluded fostherbrother.

"The words I heard screeched were the words of a spirit that had power over the soul an' body of the poor mortal that lay on the grave."

Michael recoiled as he said this, as if he would retreat from his own interpretation.

"As soon as the words were hissed," he continued, "the cold hard fingers that were tightened round my wrist—this wrist it was, and the mark of the fingers were on it a good while—were loosened, and my arm fell, benumbed like, down against my side. What I took to be a black head-stone, but what, I'm sure, was a spirit of evil, went off from me, inch by inch. Pains were in my eye-balls staring at it, and I could see it through the darkness. Then I saw it standing still, and I knew that it was close by our angel's grave. The dark spirit wasn't standing there more than a moment, when there was a frightful—a terrible cry—that near out took the senses entirely from me. Oh!—it was an awful cry, I can't well tell you what sort of cry it was."

Michael paused and reflected.

"It happened to me once," he continued after a while, "that I heard a very sorrowful cry. Going along the cliffs yonder there was a mother; a young an' comely mother she was, and there was a beautiful little boy sporting before her. And that beautiful boy raced from his mother to the edge of the cliff, and he fell over, an' he tumbled hundreds of feet down, an' he lay below, disfigured an' dead. The mother screeched, and she screeched so loud an' wild, that the fishermen on the bay, more than three miles off, heard her. But though the cry of that mother was heartrending, it wouldn't go through you like the cry in the churchyard.

"That cry was louder than the roaring of the storm. It was a great, hoarse shout, not sharp and piercing like that of the childless mother. You'd know that it came from the body of a sthrong man, and you'd know that the sthrong man was woe-begone, and you'd know that the woe-begone sthrong man, that gave the long, bewailing shout, was furious in his despair. You'd say it was the shout of a fierce madman, and that it came from a bursting heart.

"The moment I could recover from my terror, I knew that awful cry came from the sthrong man I had left lying on our angel's grave. I made my way to him, as fast as my shaking legs would bring me through the darkness. I put down my hands to touch him. He was not where he lay when I went from him. He was gone—my poor misguided fosther-brother was gone."

"Gone, Michael!—What do you mean?"

"Gone from us—gone,—gone. And the evil spirit was gone too. I could not see it anywhere, although I knew it had come and stood by the grave.

"The last Christmas-day that passed was the sixth that came and went since that night of woe. From that hour to this I never laid eyes on my poor fosther-brother, dead or alive. If the crature was a sinner, he suffered for it, and I never go to my prayers that I don't ask of the Lord that his sufferings may not go beyond this life."

CHAPTER XXXIX.

RICHARD O'MEARA'S STRANGE DISAPPEARANCE.

MICHAEL'S statement was literally true. When he had groped and stumbled to the grave of "the angel," the prostrate form of her husband was no longer there. Michael sought with his hands along the newly-erected mound; he could feel only the clammy, disjointed sodding with which the neighbours had covered it before their departure.

In the desperation of extreme terror he called aloud the name of the miserable man he had quitted only a few moments before. His summons was not replied to by the voice he wished to hear, but he was answered by the lad who had remained a watcher during Michael's absence. The boy was not on the spot where he had been when Michael parted from him. He was a short distance away, unable to make progress in the direction he wished to go, so dense was the darkness, and so numerous the obstacles. Directed by the sound of each other's voices, Michael and he felt their way to each other.

The boy's story was to this effect. Almost immediately following the departure of Michael to seek the Half-pay in the ruin, a dark form stood above the grave, and the young watcher's superstitious dread was agonizing. Some words were spoken by this mysterious visitant; the lad could only catch the sound, but not the meaning.

His father started instantly to his feet. And then it was that he screamed the harrowing cry so much dwelt on by Michael. At once, and while still shouting his despairing lament, he dashed away through the gloom.

Even in the bewilderment of his terror, the child could understand that his father had over and over again fallen in his progress through the tombs and headstones. The little fellow fearlessly endeavoured to follow. He found this impracticable, and he stood confused, and doubtful how to proceed, when Michael's shout was answered by him.

Difficult no doubt it was, and yet the Half-pay contrived to emerge from the roofless church, and join the other two. They consulted together, and Michael succeeded in descending to the town, where he provided himself with lanterns, and whence his party was reinforced by a few of the boldest of the neighbours, whose love of the marvellous overmastered their fears or stimulated their charity.

The churchyard was searched in every direction, Richard O'Meara was not in the churchyard. On his wife's fresh grave, by holding down the light, the marks of his two knees were visible, and the sodding placed loosely thereon, as the final adjustment of the mound, was found to have been displaced, as Michael explained to the examiners, when Richard O'Meara cast himself heavily upon it. The mark of the mourner's forehead could also be distinguished; and in the hollow was a pool of blood, which flowed thence along the grave's sides. Close by the little elevation a hat was found, soiled and trampled out of all shape, and thoroughly saturated with rain. This was Richard O'Meara's hat.

The neighbours agreed that the unfortunate man, bad as he was, was yet deserving of pity. It was evident that he had been bleeding profusely. And was it not a fearful thing that wherever he had gone he was bareheaded, and wounded, under the inclemency of as bleak and dreary a night as any present had ever witnessed?

Some branches broken from the trees descending the steep hill-side towards the river led to the conjecture that the missing man might have scrambled downwards in that direction. During the quest through the grove, the seekers were joined by the inhabitants of the small houses at the hill-foot. Even within their dwellings, these had been terrified by the cry uttered by Richard O'Meara. Even above the turmoil of the elements they had heard that cry.

Richard O'Meara was not in the grove on the hill-side. He was nowhere to be found.

CHAPTER XL.

THE DRUNKARD'S FATE.

THE day following was Christmas-da. It was a calm day. The storm of the night before had worn itself out, as the fury of a passionate man will become expended. The sky was clear, and frost had set in once more.

Being a holiday, the entire of the inhabitants of "The Town of the Cascades" were engaged in eager commentaries as to the probable fate of Richard O'Meara. The police were officially on the alert, prosecuting their inquiries on the same subject.

Towards midday, persons passing along the heights overhanging the eastern side of the bay near the village of the Bornochs, discovered part of a man's dress, a short distance inward from the edge of the highest cliff overlooking the sea. There was a pocket in this remnant of attire, and in this pocket letters were found, proving that it had belonged to the missing man; and Michael Hanrahan found no difficulty in identifying it as the skirt of his lost foster-brother's outside coat.

Immediately near the brow of the cliff there was no grass, and the bare soil, partly clay and partly pulverized rock, was soft and yielding, rendered particularly so by the recent heavy snow and rain. Here numerous footprints were distinctly visible, and it was particularly noticed that the mark of the right foot was that of a boot or shoe, while the indent recognized for the print of the left was that of a stocking without other covering. The police did not overlook so evident a tracing. A pair of boots belonging to Richard O'Meara were obtained at the cottage: one of these corresponded accurately with the imprint of the right foot.

There could be no doubt but that the despairing Richard O'Meara had—wonderful to relate

—made his way to the towering cliff at hand, and had thence flung himself headlong into the roaring waves below. The wind had blown inland from the south the night before, and the inhabitants of the little bathing-place pronounced, one and all, that a more violent storm had never uplifted the waters of the bay, that the lower portions of the village had been deluged, and that the waves must have lashed the cliff half way to its summit, when the fearful plunge was made.

Mingled with the human footprints near the cliff were the impressions made by the paws of a dog. A large dog the animal must have been.

When Michael Hanrahan had left his "angel's" grave on the previous night, the dog Teague was there, close by his master's outstretched body. Teague was not to be found from the moment of his master's disappearance. It was plain the attached brute had followed Richard O'Meara to the cliff, and that, self-devoted, he had shared his master's fate. They had plunged together into the sea.

CHAPTER XLI.

LAST TRACES.

"What is the distance, Michael, from the church-yard on the hill to the cliff where the last traces of your unhappy foster-brother were found?"

"It is over an' above two long Irish miles, as the crow would fly, and as poor Dick O'Meara went."

"As I viewed the country from the hill-top, it appears to me next to an impossibility that even in the broad daylight any one could take a direct course over such ground. That the track could be followed on the night you have described would be nothing short of the miraculous. There is a road—he must have gone by the road."

"Poor crature! he did not take to the road.

And 'twas as you say, miraculous, how he could have made to the cliff the way he went. Let your own self set out from the churchyard any day, the brightest that ever shone, and travel the exact ground he took, at your ease an' your leisure, and nothing to throuble you, and if you don't give it up before half the journey is done, I'm mistaken greatly."

"And yet you say he did not go along the road?"

"Of a surety he did not, and I'll tell you why I say that so positively.

"When the search was over for him, and that we made sure of the untimely end of himself—Lord be good to his sowl!—and of our loving dog, I went here and there myself to pick out marks of him. I didn't say to any one but Mary where I was going, or what I was about. But let them talk as they liked, I couldn't get the love for my fosther-brother out of my heart, and so I made a pilgrimage like afther him.

"I went my way while the marks were fresh. Sometimes I found tracks of the dog, sometimes of himself, the mark of his feet, or bits or shreds of his clothes. And so I thravelled on and on. Parts of the way I couldn't follow all out. Although I was at the time an active chap enough of my age, I couldn't swim the river in my clothes; I couldn't throw myself down forty feet or more of a rock, as he did, where there was no resting-place for the foot to fasten; I couldn't climb up rocks straight and smooth as a plastered wall, as sure marks showed me he did. But up the steep hills I went, and down in the deep hollows below them I went, tracking him all along. Through bogs where I sank knee-deep I went, over hedges, and dhrains, and ditches I went, tracking him all the time surely. Do you see that snarling hill over yonder?"

"All I see is hill and hollow; but you mean the hill with the craggy brow rising suddenly above the less prominent acclivities?"

"Send your look by the corner of the white-washed house with the rick of turf close by it."

"I see the hill you point to."

"That hill with the snarling back is called *Ard-na-Cuillagh.*"

"Give me the English of *Ard-na-Cuillagh*, Michael."

"*Ard-na-Cuillagh* means 'The High Grove.' There is no grove there now, but in the old times, as the ancient people say, it was all a wood over this counthry as far as the eye can go, and the wood on *Ard-na-Cuillagh* was high above the rest. Over that hill of *Ard-na-Cuillagh* the poor fellow crossed, as I'll make sure to you.

"When you mount to the brow of *Ard-na-Cuillagh*, and you go down a little way along its side nearest to the sea, mind yourself well; if you do not, down you plunge headlong into a deep quarry, and if you escape the fall you'll have the luck of a four-leaved shamrock. Hard grown bushes, sprouting from the roots of the trees that were there long ago, and briars, and blackberry brambles hide the quarry from you until you're on it. You are minding me?"

"I am, attentively."

"Guided by my marks, I crossed the hill of *Ard-na-Cuillagh.* I knew there was a quarry on its side, and I had the daylight, and I was careful. I stood on the brow and looked down. On one of the hard grown bushes I saw something I thought I ought to know; I scrambled for it, and I got it. It was one of the boots worn by the poor lost crature when he disappeared from the churchyard. The boot of the left foot it was."

"Ha! the mark of the left foot above the cliff was that of a stocking, you said?"

"You are right enough. 'Lord be good to me,' I said to myself, 'he must have tumbled head foremost into the quarry. If it was not for the fastening of his foot in the tough branches here, he would not have ended his life in the sea; he would never have gone beyond this.'

"The fall down was stopped when his left foot was entangled in the fork of the bush; and when the boot parted from him in his struggle to get free, the bottom of the quarry was not far distant from him. But"—added Michael in a broken voice—"the poor crature must have been sorely mangled and disfigured."

"It is evident from your statement, Michael, that the ill-doomed man did not follow the road when he left the churchyard, and that he must have made his way, over almost insurmountable obstacles, to the fatal cliff."

Michael looked round in apprehension of a listener. The movement was, however, no more than an expression of the confidence he placed in me.

"I said to you before what I now say to you again. It was my judgment at the time, and it is my judgment still, afther six years' thinking of it over,—if when the last prayers were said over the angel's grave, and that he knelt at the grave's head, he had not stopped short in the blessing of himself—meaning by that that he gave up hope in God—if he had finished the signing of the cross on himself, and had humbly called on the Holy Trinity for protection, the spirit of evil that stood in the churchyard would not have got the power over him to carry him along where no Christian could find footing through the darkness, without a spirit's help. And he would not have been dhragged along by the evil spirit to his desthruction."

I agree in Michael's doctrine, although I may doubt the reality of its exemplification in this instance. For we know that by the God of mercy the greatest sinners are forbidden to despair.

CHAPTER XLII.

CONCLUSION.

"A good morning to you, Mary."

Mary glanced up at me from her "cobbey-house" in the cliff, the never-absent smile greeting me.

"Are you there, Sir? A bright good morning to you. Come down here, an' roost yourself comfortably."

I accepted Mary's invitation, and took my accustomed seat beside her.

"Well, Sir, you have something to ask me. I know by your face that you have."

"I came for the purpose of making some inquiries certainly."

"So I bethought me. Well, Sir, here I am,

ready an' willing to answer you. 'Tis a great blessing that we can stitch an' talk at the same time. We don't dhrive the needle with the tongue, to be sure,—but I think it goes the merrier when the tongue is busy."

"I presume, Mary, that you changed your name, and were married to Michael Hanrahan shortly after Richard O'Meara's death?"

"'Deed then 'tis no presumption in you to say that, because it was just what turned out. Michael an' myself were a long time coorting, as you know by this time. 'Tis a positive proof that we were taken with one another all out entirely, or we'd never have the patience to wait so long. We'd fight, maybe, an' part company, if our two hearts were not in it, an' if it wasn't *sa creeveen sha* with us. The one of us said to the other in the beginning that we wouldn't be man an' wife while we were so poor entirely, an' nobody to give us a start."

"Your father and mother had no fortune to bestow on you, Mary?"

"I was an orphan girl," answered Mary, "an'

Michael was an orphan boy. 'Twas much of a muchness between us in that way, an' there could be no scrambling for the sake of lucre anyhow— Upon my word," she continued, "when Michael an' I danced the first jig together (it was his beautiful dancing that bewildered me about him), we hadn't so much between us as would pay the piper for his music."

Mary laughed outright at her account of her own and Michael's poverty when Michael jigged himself into her maiden affections.

"But—" Mary checked herself in her glee—"it was wrong of me to say it was the dancing that took the heart from me, and gave it to Michael. It was the dancing first made me cotton to him certainly. But when I came to know him, the more I knew of him the betther I thought of him. It wasn't for the dancing all out that I loved my poor Michael; it wasn't for his beauty either—he hadn't over an' above to spare of that at any time. I loved Michael because he was honest and tendher-hearted; I loved him because it was he knew how to give the good advice when I'd be giddy; I loved him because he was a wise boy; I loved him because he was a good Christian. The priest himself couldn't be a betther Christian than Michael was, an' is to the moment. An'—"

Mary's smile now was one of warm affection, irradiating her comely features directly from the heart.

"An' I loved my poor Michael because Michael loved me;—ay indeed did he, with the whole of his heart. He loved me betther than any one else could, the poor fellow. There was no deception in Michael.

"Well, my dear, what would you have of it? As I tould you, we made up our minds not to be man an' wife while we were so poor entirely that we were forced to go in score with the piper that played our first jig together for us.

"Richard O'Meara—Heaven's rest be to his soul!—owed Michael a good sum, an' I put by my wages for years. We made up our minds to open a sthrong huxther's shop in the town beyand, an' to live like a lord an' a lady on our profits. But when the poor misthress was sick an' in need, my little *caubogue* of a gathering went away bit by bit. We couldn't see her wanting while we had it to give her. An' what Richard O'Meara left behind him wouldn't pay the tithe of what he owed to sthrangers, an' Michael an' I said we wouldn't put out our hands to make a grab, and let the sthrangers go empty-handed. So when the bitther misfortune fell on the cottage an' all that lived there, the two of us were low enough, you may be sure.

"Michael looked at me sorrowfully with tears in his eyes. 'What are we to do now, Mary?' he asked of me. 'I'll tell you what we'll do, Michael,' I made answer. 'Here's a thirty-shilling note; it's all we have between us. We'll get married on the strength of the thirty shillings, an' we'll put our trust in God for the time to come,' says I."

"And you married 'on the strength of the thirty-shilling note?'—and you did not establish the 'strong huxter's shop?'"

"Ha, ha, ha!—Huxter's shop, indeed! When

our marriage fee was paid—(for we made no poor mouths to the priest, an' went to it as hearty an' as lofty-headed as if we were the owners of thousands) —when our marriage-fee was paid, an' when we bought our wedding-supper, there wasn't much left to set up the huxter's shop with. 'We'll put our trust in God,' I said to Michael;—an' God didn't desert us. 'Tis a truth, to be sure, that from the very first day we belonged to one another, the current was sthrong against us. But didn't I help Michael, an' didn't Michael help Mary, with *a graw* an' a good will? Indeed we did! I often thought that the scramble we had to make, arm-in-arm, an' shouldher to shouldher, gave us a faith an' a trust in each other we might want if the huxter's shop was making a fortune for us. Howsomever, my honest, loving Michael an' his Mary are contented with their lot. They wouldn't swap husbands or wives with any one, and they're thankful to God for his blessings."

I reverenced Mary's pious and cheerful acquiescence in the decree that assigned her a life of struggle and privation ;—this acquiescence evidenced by her look upward, and by her smile of resignation.

She gave me some details descriptive of her matrimonial voyage of six years' duration. Although from the port of departure with the remnant of the "thirty-shilling note" as sea-store, there had been a constant buffet against wave and tide, yet there she was, in her "cobbey-house" in the cliff, ready to dispense what she called "her rusty water" for a very precarious remuneration, while she patched a cravat for Michael, without a frown on her brow, or a murmur of discontent from her lips. On the contrary, she smiled ever—ever.

Very many there are of high station and with the dowry of princesses who might envy her.

"I believe, Mary, the Colonel, as you called him, does not live hereabouts at present. I have not seen him since I took up my residence among the Bornochs, and I think I must have recognized him had I met him, so accurate have been your descriptions and Michael's of him."

"You are right enough, Sir, by my word. He is not here, not a bit of him, an' no one in this part of the world can tell what became of him."

"How is that, Mary?"

"I gave you a history before now of one Bridget Scallon, the woman that kept house for the three neighbours above the bridge. Well, my dear, it was the third night after the Christmas-day when Richard O'Meara's fate was made known, that Bridget Scallon heard the thump of the Colonel's leg above stairs an' down stairs, an' here and there about the house. She was in her kitchen, taking her good, sthrong tay. I tould you how she managed to give it the sthrength."

"You did. I remember how it was that Bridget contrived to convert weak tea into strong tea."

"Well, she didn't disturb herself, poor woman,—the tay was too good. The Curnel's ways were so curious at all times that she didn't stir to look afther him. When the fourth cup was finished, she sat on her stool before the bright turf fire, an' she fell fast asleep. No blame to Bridget; she seldom got a doze in her bed. She was woke up by some one shaking her as if she was a sack of potatoes that wanted packing. It was the Curnel; he had her by the shouldher, an' he was rattling her bones in their sockets.

"'Up—shut—the—door,' says the Curnel to Bridget." Mary's imitation of the Half-pay's gruff, abrupt address was amusing.

"Bridget found it hard to bruise the sthrong tay from her eyes with her knuckles.

"'Shut—the—door!' says the Curnel again. Bridget Scallon followed afther him, by her own account, in a kind of a maze. Bridget's 'sthrong tay' would often make her like one that was fairy sthruck. The Curnel went out into the winter's night, Bridget shut the door, an' then went back to finish her nap before the kitchen-fire. From that hour to this neither Bridget, nor Michael, nor Toby Purcell, nor any of them could find out where our poor Curnel went. As queer, but as honest-hearted a Curnel he was as any one could know."

"Never seen or heard of since, Mary?"

"He was seen once, an' once for all. The day didn't break the morning after Bridget shut him out until it was beyond seven o'clock. As the day came in, Pat Mulhearn, the carman, coming with goods to the town, met him full twenty miles away. He was punching along the road at a hard rate, an' there was a knapsack, the same that soldiers wear, sthrapped between his shoulders. Walking at his best by the side of the Curnel was a boy of about thirteen years of age. What boy was that, do you think?"

"Let me see. Richard O'Meara's son!"

"The very same it was. Young Dick O'Meara wasn't seen in our town ever since, no more than the Curnel. But I ought to take up my word. The Curnel an' the boy were heard of again in a manner, I may say. Three years afther they took a French leave of us a sthrange man came here, a stone-cutter by thrade he was, as he made known to us. He came to Michael, an' Michael went with him, an' showed him the grave of Richard O'Meara's wife. This sthrange stone-cutter fell to work, an' he put over the grave the tomb where you prayed a prayer the first day I met you, if you remember it."

"I do remember the circumstance, Mary."

"Well, the sthranger wouldn't tell who sent him, or where he came from, but we knew from the printing on the tomb who was to be his paymasther. As soon as his job was finished, the sthrange stone-cutter set off with himself, leaving us to guesswork. And so, sir, you have all we know about our Curnel and young Dick O'Meara. You'd like to learn news of others, maybe."

"Yes, Mary, I came here specially to acquire that knowledge. Ned Culkin—and Tom O'Loughlin—where are they?"

"The workhouse is between this spot where we are and the town. If you go there, an' go into the place where they shut up the sick people that haven't house or home of their own, nor any one to care for them, there you'll find Ned Culkin. Toby Purcell had some joke about him that Michael repeated to me, an' that used to make the neighbours laugh, but

Michael and myself could see no joke in it, and Michael said it wasn't charity to make merry over the misfortunes of others."

"Do you happen to remember Toby Purcell's joke, Mary?"

"I do. It was something about Ned Culkin being a gauger, an' losing entirely the use of his limbs. 'How do you prove that Ned Culkin is a broken gauger?' Toby Purcell would ask of some one. An' when they'd be thinking an' thinking, he'd give the answer himself, an' you'd suppose by him that he said something comical. 'I'll tell you,' Toby would say, 'because he has lost his walk.'"

"A very lame jest of Toby Purcell's, Mary."

"It is you I believe. If you have a fancy to visit Ned Culkin lying without the power to put his limbs undher him, the door of the workhouse will be opened for you by a shrivelled up 'natomy of a little elderly man, with his shoulders up to his ears, an' his two hands rubbing each other ever an' always. If you look at him you'll see all that's left of the decayed gentleman."

"One other person I wish to hear of—Nora Spruhan?"

"Before I tell you of Nora Spruhan, let your own eyes bear witness for you. Get up an' go a little distance farther along the cliffs. Walk on until you come to the highest cliff above the bay. If I don't mistake very much, you'll see a woman sitting on the very brow of that high cliff. You'll know that she isn't old, an' you'll wondher if she can be young; go an' see her for yourself. If you have money about you, bestow on her an alms: she won't crave from you, but she will take it if you offer it. Poor crature, she is in need of charity. When you come back I will tell you all you will want to know about Nora Spruhan."

I followed Mary's instructions, and reached the spot she had indicated. There, as she had foretold, a female was sitting on the far-projecting ledge of a rock that overhung the bay. The sea boomed sullenly two hundred feet below.

Her person was wrapped in a long, tattered, blue mantle, such as the Irish peasantry of the old school wear. The hood of this mantle was on her head, her bare feet dangled over the precipice. Her body was bent forwards, and though her face was hidden from me, I could perceive that she was gazing straight forward, out to sea. She did not note or heed my footsteps as I approached. I bade her good-day. She did not return my salutation, but she turned her head and looked vacantly at me, without inquiry or interest in her sunken black eyes. While she looked, I saw that her cheeks were hollow and without colour, save that of sunburn and exposure. Her full lips were close, and there were lines down from them, expressive of settled melancholy. Her jetty hair flowed uncared for from beneath her hood, covering her forehead, and partially her face: I held some money towards her; the arm protruded from her shrouding mantle was wasted and shrivelled. She made no acknowledgment of the gift, but holding it fast clutched, she gathered the mantle round her again, and resumed her outward gaze as before.

"Have you seen her?" Mary asked, as I rejoined her.

"I have, Mary. If this be Nora Spruhan, I could trace few remains of the beauty you have described. She is an object of compassion."

"To be pitied she is. Well, the crature you saw is Nora Spruhan. From the time of Richard O'Meara's loss, her reason went. She said to Michael that she had caused his downfall, and that his ghost haunted her. She creeps about the town an' counthry, speaking little to any one. She would not seek for a roof to cover her at night, but people bring her in an' shelther her. She never asks for charity, but she will take what is given her. Whatever she receives in the day she will leave where she is lodged an' fed at night. She spends most of her time sitting where you found her. It is the spot from which Richard O'Meara plunged to his death. It is said she spends the night there, if no charitable neighbour gives her the covering of a roof. If Nora Spruhan was not what she ought to be, 'tis God's will that she suffers for it here, and my prayer is that He will be good to her hereafter."

A SEQUEL TO MY NARRATIVE.

CHAPTER EXPLANATORY.

The term of my vacation having expired, I quitted the Bornoch village to resume my home duties. By-the-way, I would recommend such of my friends as are not over-fastidious about accommodation and so forth to become "*Forneyaghs*" by all means for a few weeks of the autumn, and I venture to promise them a return home with renovated health.

When I ceased to be a Forneyagh, it was with the impression that I was bidding a final farewell to my friend, the anomalous Michael Hanrahan, and to his cheery-hearted Mary. But in this supposition I was mistaken.

Some years subsequently, when again quitting my daily labours for my short holiday, I journeyed through a different part of the country, at the opposite extremity of Ireland, I may say.

I was seated on one of those exclusively Irish conveyances, an "outside car." I had, for some time, been passing an enclosed demesne. Here and there I could obtain glimpses of the grounds. I could see grassy hillocks, and declivities, some sun-lighted, some in shadow, and the shadow passing off and giving place to sunlight, and again the sunny spots dimmed by shadows, as the autumn clouds sailed on. On an elevation a short distance from the road, there was a mansion not of recent erection, as the style of architecture told. It was surrounded by noble, aristocratic trees; woods mounted behind the house,—ancient woods they appeared to be,—and I caught the reflection of the brilliant but not oppressive sun, in a river that flowed below it.

I enjoyed so vividly the rich and varied landscape on either side, that I proceeded at a leisurely pace, permitting the horse to poke his head downward that he might relieve the hitherto erect position of his neck, and yawn away the tugging of the bit.

Approaching the entrance gate to the demesne and mansion I had been admiring, I observed a person in advance of me, whose almost unique personalities at once arrested my attention.

"Can it be possible?" was my self-inquiry. "*Can* this be my Bornoch acquaintance, the waiter of the little hotel there; my well-individualized and esteemed crony, Michael Hanrahan?"

The person thus speculated on walked directly from me; his back towards me. He was low in stature; Michael Hanrahan was of the same elevation to a hair. When Michael Hanrahan walked, there was a wabble at the knee-joints, an imperfect fitting of the boles and sockets thereabouts producing, as I judged, this peculiar suppleness of limb. The knee-joints of the person before me rolled in the sockets also. The head somewhat inclined to the right shoulder was Michael Hanrahan's method of wearing his head too. In his capacity of waiter, I had never but once seen a hat or a cap on

Michael Hanrahan: Michael's hair was jet-black, abundant, and lank. The little fellow I examined was bareheaded, his hair was jet-black, abundant, and lank. I was almost certain of my man.

But there was one peculiarity of movement not identical. The individual I surveyed swayed his body very much to the right and left as he progressed. Michael Hanrahan, during my intimacy with him, did not carry himself so.

But what could this possibly be hanging pendant from the left shoulder of this three-fourths yes, and one-fourth no, Michael Hanrahan, which swayed pendulum like with the motion of the bearer?

I descended from my "outside car," directing the driver to remain stationary, and I advanced as noiselessly as I could to take close scrutiny. When near enough for certainty, I discovered to my surprise, that the pendant object was a pudding-shaped sack, above which a diminutive human face, and two diminutive hands protruded. The bearer of this fardel was singing.

"Michael Hanrahan's goldfinch quaver to a dead

certainty!" I assured myself. I could not at the moment catch distinctly the words of the ditty, but I was favoured with them subsequently. The air was a lullaby, and there was a mingling of drollery and pathos in it.

The vocalist turned short round. Down his breast, from the left shoulder also, was a second pudding-shaped sack, and above it a second diminutive face, and a second pair of diminutive hands. Michael Hanrahan, the veritable Michael Hanrahan, of the Bornoch village, confronted me not four paces distant.

He stopped, opened his large grey eyes wide, and stared at me. Then his capacious mouth expanded right and left, to an almost fabulous extent, to produce a smile of recognition.

"As I hope for mercy," he exclaimed, raising both his hands; "it is nobody else but Mr. ——— that I see standing there fornent me,—nobody else but himself. Oh, then! ain't I proud entirely to see you not looking an hour owlder than you were this time four years. Faith, I'm proud entirely."

Michael and I shook hands; our greeting was cordial. I esteemed Michael, and Michael was attached to me.

"Michael Hanrahan," I said, and I could not control my laughter while I put my question, "this is an odd kind of harness I see on you. Where to, in the name of goodness, are you conveying the children, and why in this singular manner?"

"I'm nursing, as in duty bound, and as all tendher parients ought to do. They're a brace o twins, Sir, if you plaise. This little crature" — gently smoothing the head surmounting the sack in front—"belongs to the faymale sex. And this" —turning his back that I might view the other— "is a little boy, God bless it. They were sent into the world, Lord be praised for all his blessings, hot-foot, the one afther the other. Mary here is the eldest, by five minutes or so, an' for that raison she's to the front along my heart. Michael, here behind, is by coorse the youngest, by five minutes or so."

He put himself into the wavy motion I had

noticed as not identical with the Michael Hanrahan I had known, and he crooned the lullaby I had before heard :—

> "Och mavrone! that ever I married;—
> It leaves me here for to sigh an' to weep,—
> Moaning an' groaning an' rocking the cradle,
> An' plaising a child that won't go to sleep."

There was a cool waggery in Michael's manner, while he affected seriousness, that stimulated my mirth again.

"I'll be thankful if you don't laugh so hearty, Sir," he expostulated; "or you'll rouse up the twins. If it cost you as much as it cost me to shut their eyes, I go bail you wouldn't shout so loud. Huzz-o-o—Huz-zoo-oo-oo!—

> "Och mavrone, etc."

"Well, Michael, excuse me. But positively, the novelty of your contrivance, for which you certainly deserve a patent, and your manner of explanation are too provocative. But I will laugh underhand."

And suiting the action to the word, I placed both

my hands before my face, and laughed *sotto voce* until I was satisfied.

"Undher hand sure enough, by gor," I heard Michael remark; and as I removed my veil I saw that he himself was grimacing at a furious rate, in his endeavour to control his mirth.

"I'll tell you honestly how the bright notion came into my head," said Michael.

"They wanted Mary up at the house very bad, Mary is their brains-carrier, you must know. 'Michael,' she says to me, wriggling her head, and shaking her fist within an inch of my nose,—'Michael,' she says, 'mind the childre well while I'm from them. If you don't, I'll blacken the eye in your head when I come back.' An' with that, off she set. To keep my eye from being bulged out, I took on to do Mary's bidding. Ullaloo! if it wasn't an out-of-the-way job she gave me. Chickens don't take to the cock, somehow. They tossed an' they tumbled, an' they clawed at aich other in the cradle, an' the squallin' of 'em brought the tears into my eyes:—I found out that the cock can cry over the chickens though he can't cluck for 'em rightly. 'Come,' says I, 'in the name of the Lord I'll thry a way of my own with ye.' I took the throwsers out of the box, and I measured the childre to it to a nicety. Mary is a quarther of an inch lengthier than Michael,—she grew that much in the five minutes start that she had. I tied the legs of the throwsers, as you may behold, to match their size. I scrooged Mary into this leg an' Michael into the other; you'd think 'twas into Paradise they got, when 'twas only into the legs of the throwsers they were squeezed. I slung 'em over my shouldher, as you may observe; I sang my croonawn for them, rocking them as I marched, hither an' thither, in the way you saw. And aren't they in a nate, natural sleep, the poor things,—aren't they, now?"

"You have succeeded admirably, Michael, in your experiment at clucking."

"I think 'twas worth your while to come the long journey you took, Sir, to bring the plan home with you."

"So it was, Michael."

"And I think Mary won't make war against my eye with her great big fist, that isn't much over twice the size of her weeny namesake's fist."

Michael inserted his forefinger against the tiny palm of the infant Mary's hand, which hung drooping down from her "leg of the throwsers," and although the little head hung to one side helplessly, still the sleeping child acknowledged the object of its touch by grasping it.

"Well, well, well," Michael said, as gently and as tenderly as if he had ceased to be the crowing, strutting chanticleer, and had been transformed into the plaintive, motherly hen of the "brace of twins,"—"Well, well, well, little doowshy Mary, you have the love for me, I do think. You have the very features of the other Mary, an' 'tis my prayer for you that you may be like her in every way, within an' without. May God be your safeguard, my weeshy child, and grant you his grace. An' may you grow up as comely an' as good as the mother that bore you."

Michael laid his cheek gently on the drooping head of the infant he apostrophized. He raised it again, and cautiously holding up the finger round which those of the baby had twined,—

"Isn't that very purty—very purty, Sir?" he asked. "It puts me in mind of the woodbine that is too puny to hold up its own head, an' that twines round the stout bush to support it.

"Ay," he continued, following out his simple comparison,—"and that rewards the support it gets by bedizening the bush it creeps through with bunches of flowers, pleasant to the eye an' sweet smelling."

Michael's paternal affection, and Michael's rather poetical expression of it, made me almost forget the ludicrousness of his nursing accoutrements.

"I little expected, Michael, to meet you here, fully two hundred miles from the spot where I left you when I bade good-bye to you and the bornochs."

"And I had no more notion at that time, Sir, of standing on this spot, than I had of flying sky-high. Little did I think at the time that I'd be so well off at the present day. Mary and myself live here in the lodge inside the gate. We have a beautiful garden; we have cattle an' sheep on the demesne; we have fine wages; plenty within and without we have, as you may partly see;" and Michael looked down at Mary as she slept along his breast, and glanced over his shoulder at the junior Michael on his back.

"And Mary?—she is as well, I hope, and I dare say as handsome and as cheerful, as when she and I were such close friends?"

"The Lord bless you, Sir, Mary is out-an'-out more blooming and more comely than the day we married, and 'twould not be easy to match her then. As slick as a mouse, and as plump as a partridge, Mary is. She was neat an' tidy when she was obliged to wear the wrong side of the gown turned out the week days, to have the right side clane for Sunday,—and when the legs were bare six days out of the seven, to make the stockings hold out for going to mass. Now 'twould pleasure you to look at her in her new feathers after the moulting. Mary an' myself had a hard tussle with poverty unbeknown to the world. She didn't repine, and she had a cheerful heart in our blackest days. And God has rewarded her for being satisfied with His will."

"You were not jealous, Michael, of the intimate terms I was on with your Mary?"

"Ho, ho, ho!—jealous inagh!—jealous of Mary? I didn't care if the bravest, an' best-bedizened, an' best-looking buck that ever made it the business of his life to delude faymales,—and such there are in plenty, as I happen to know,—was to make up to Mary. Mary would be the one to show my gallant hero his distance. Mary is a good Christian an' a faithful wife."

Michael paused a moment, and his mouth expanded.

"More be token," he added, "she was safe enough with you. You wern't over young, Sir, and—"

Michael left this sentence unfinished, but he cast his eye from my figure to his own, in evident self-appreciation—comfortably satisfied that personal appearance was all in his own favour.

"Michael!—Michael!—Michael!—"

A female voice, thrice calling Michael's name here interrupted our conversation.

"Now," said Michael, with a self-approving expansion of the lips, and a shrewd wink at me, "now for the blackening of my eye with the heavy fist."

Mary, with a look of consternation, made her appearance outside the entrance gate. She held forth both her hands beseechingly.

"Michael, Michael, Michael!" she again cried, "where are the childre?—What did you do with them?"

Michael advanced towards her at a leisurely pace, rocking his body, thereby to see-saw the children, singing as he went:—

"Och mavrone! that ever I married;—
It laves me here for to sigh an' to weep,—
Moaning an' groaning an' rocking the cradle,
An' plaising a child that won't go to sleep."

I looked on at the meeting between Michael and Mary. The former did not seem to apprehend the threatened attack on his eye; he went directly on as I have described. Mary gazed at him as he approached, her hands still extended. There was a conviction that the "childre" were safe, but a puzzle as to the reason for her conviction. When Michael came close to her, still singing his lullaby, the two extended hands smote each other rapidly, somewhat in the spirit of the delighted applause bestowed in theatres on successful artistes. And Mary's laugh, coming from the heart, rang clear and musical. If you are within earshot of merry laughter that has nothing mocking or ill-natured in it, even although you be ignorant of the incentive, you feel compelled to join chorus—just as you yawn involuntarily for companionship. And my laughter mingled with Mary's. Still Michael was, to all appearance, serious. I saw him carefully remove "the brace of twins" from his own to Mary's shoulder, Mary accommodating herself to receive the load, her gleeish laughter still continuing. Young Mary and young Michael were awakened from their "nate, natural sleep" by their mother's outgiven mirth. They were extracted from their imprisonment, not without management, Michael holding on at the extremity of the trousers' legs while Mary drew forth her offspring. They were lodged safely in her arms, where they nestled.

It was only now my presence was recognized, and Mary advanced to me blithely. Both her arms were clasped round "the brace of twins," and they crossed over each other at the wrists.

"If you *must* shake my hands, Sir," she said, her laughter subsiding to a bland, happy smile, "you'll have to take them cross-barred as they are. Indeed an' indeed, it makes me glad to see you, and to see you so well."

Beyond a question Mary justified Michael's boast. Michael went as far back as the day of his marriage;—whatever she might then have been, she was now "more blooming and more comely" certainly, than she had been when her contribution to the household revenue arose from her dispensation of "rusty water" to the Forneyaghs who sought it.

From her snow-white muslin cap, decorated tastily with glossy pink ribbons,—which cap, by-the-way, was fixed on with ever-so-little of a coquettish to-one-sidedness,—from this saucy little cap down to her spotless white stockings and neatly-fitting, well-polished shoes (Michael was famous in his capacity of "boots"), there was that visible care of arrangement, and that becomingness of attire, which, while displaying her embonpoint to advantage, was a direct indication of a well-arranged mind.

If, to use Michael's language again, while she and the same Michael had had "a hard tussle with poverty" there was ever a smile of resignation and peace, often of innocent merriment, on Mary's face, the smile was now radiant, as well it might be, seeing that she had now a wren's nest of a house to live in, good wages, a beautiful garden, and grass on the demesne for as many head of sheep and cattle as she and Michael could collect. Oh! Mary and Michael were a wealthy and a happy couple indeed.

While I shook her hands so cautiously as not to

disturb the twins, I caught Michael's proud eye travelling from his Mary to me, and from me to his Mary, with the easy-to-be-understood query beaming from it.

"Well, Sir, and what do you think of Mary now?"

And I did not fail to exchange with Michael a glance which meant—

"I wish you joy, Michael, of your brace of twins, and I congratulate you on the possession of their blooming nurse."

I need scarcely say that up to this, being ignorant of the means by which my honest friends had progressed to such an enviable and unanticipated point of elevation, I was anxious to learn how their fortunes had so altered.

There was a considerable town within half a mile of our place of meeting. I put up my quarters there for two days, at the request of Mary and Michael;—during that time my curiosity was satisfied.

The history of Michael and his Mary's prosperity, is, properly speaking, an addendum to the preceding narrative of a drunkard's career. I will therefore add what I learned during my stay, by way of Sequel.

SEQUEL.—CHAPTER I.

THE DARK BEGGAR-MAN ON THE BRIDGE.

It was the eve of Christmas-day.

On Christmas-eve, nine years antecedent to the occurrences taken up as a sequel, the body of Ellen O'Meara had been laid in the hill-top churchyard, overlooking what I have called "The Town of the Cascades." Nine years antecedent, Ellen O'Meara's erring widower had made his way over almost insurmountable obstacles, taking into account the murkiness and inclemency of the night, to the highest cliff overhanging the "Bornoch" bay.

Within half a mile or so of the lodge wherein, after a lapse of three years, I found Michael Hanrahan and his Mary so prosperously and so enviably located, was the large county town of ——. This county town was nearly two hundred good Irish miles distant from "The Town of the Cascades." Its name or its locality I am not at liberty to indicate.

The county town of —— was divided into two unequal portions by a broad, pellucid river, which flowed through it after passing what I will take the liberty of calling the Mansion house of Michael and Mary Hanrahan. This river I had noticed glittering in the sunlight, below the house, while I made my observations from the road.

It was, as I have said, the eve of Christmas-day, and this particular Christmas-eve fell on a Wednesday. Wednesday was also a market day in the county town of ——, and from both causes the town was full of busy people.

From the surrounding country district, the peasantry, in particular the female peasantry, thronged in with carts and baskets full of turkeys, geese, ducks, young cocks, and pullets. The turkeys as they progressed through the bewildering continuation of houses, through the bustle around them, and through the constant succession of strange faces, gazed about in silent wonder. The geese often screamed angrily, and often gabbled impatiently, as they delivered their opinions touching the strange and unwelcome sights they were compelled to witness. The ducks made frequent loud expostulations as they were borne along. The cocks were often clamorous and indignant; but the pullets, sleek of feather, were for the most part sad and dejected,—Turkeys, geese, ducks, cocks, and pullets were all puzzled, however, to comprehend why they had been rudely manacled, why they had been fettered in ill-assorted pairs (always the case), and why they had been forced, without reference to their wishes, to visit such unimagined and such uncongenial scenes.

Alas! their prevoyance had not enabled them to foresee the drift of all the attention to their appetites, their likings, and their comforts, hitherto bestowed on them. They knew not at the time that this was all selfishness and deception on the part of those they regarded as disinterested, fast friends; that all this apparent kindliness was nothing more than a hypocritical prelude to their destination as regal Christmas fare on the tables of the residents of their county town.

A providential shortsightedness was theirs: had they been endowed with prescience, they would not have disported through their native fields, their native streams, their ponds, their farmyards. Let us ask ourselves how many of us act more in accordance with our premonitive superiority.

The markets of the county town were largely supplied with other rural produce, exclusive of the betrayed feathered visitants; the shops were busy, one and all; and throughout the short winter day, as fast as sales were made and purchases perfected, every road leading countrywards was alive and merry with the returners home, freighted with Christmas fare and Christmas presents for their own firesides.

A bridge and a blind man, or dark man, as we say in Ireland, have been associated in my mind from my earliest childhood. All who have read that book of books, the Arabian Nights' Entertainment, will bear in mind that on the bridge of Bagdad, in the extreme east, and at a distant day, a dark man had located himself to crave alms. Here in the extreme west of Europe, and up to a very recent period, there was scarce one bridge connected with a town, or even village, untenanted by its own dark man. And the association between the bridge and the blind man is of such long standing with me, that I cannot help feeling as I pass a bridge, as if it were denuded of its furniture, and not to the full extent fulfilling the purpose of its erection, when no "dark man" is there to urge his beggar's petition.

On the particular Christmas-eve now to be recorded, not less than three "dark men," had at an early hour of the day taken their station on the bridge of the county town of ——, to receive the alms so liberally dispensed by the incessant stream of passengers. At Christmas the gripe even of the miserly relaxes somewhat, while the hand of the benevolent opens freely, and shares to the utmost extent of means with the needy.

In the beggar's profession, as in all professions, there is a gradus and a status. Even with beggars there is a field for the development of talent, and a scope for the flight of genius. And there are to be found practising the craft, mere matter-of-fact beggars, beggars beyond mediocrity, and beggars of distinction in their calling. Further,—there is a scintillation of poetry from the Irish character, confined to no rank, and eliminating under all imaginable phases. So that the eminent Irish beggar is, for the most part, a poetic beggar also.

Properly speaking, the sequel of my narrative has connection with only one of the dark men on the bridge of the county town of ——, yet for the sake of contrast I am led to notice the other two.

At the ascent of the bridge, at one end, a low and somewhat corpulent dark man, with a round, ruddy face, deeply indented by the disease that in childhood had deprived him of sight, was placed. He knelt humbly on a boss, or round stool formed of straw. He supported himself in this position by leaning with one hand on his long and stout professional staff, while in the other he held a wooden platter to receive the Christmas offerings. A benevolent observer, while searching for a halfpenny to lay on the platter, noticed to another similarly occupied that the dark man must not have been at home when he was measured for his coat. The friend to whom the remark was made understood it to mean, either that the garment had been put together without even a remote reference to the height or bulk of the wearer, or that it had been cut to the measure of some one ever so much taller and bulkier than its present occupant. The coat so criticised was of the stoutest and warmest grey frieze; its tails extended considerably beyond the heels of the dark man as he knelt and rested in the puddle. The collar rose so high at the back of his head as nearly to displace the battered hat above it; the wooden skewer which should have fastened it in front was under his right arm, and the sleeves were turned back as far as the elbows, to permit the protrusion of the hands.

This dark man was not eminent in his profession. His appeal of "Give a charity to the blind" was repeated over and over again. No variety of words, or change of intonation. Yet let merit be given where merit is due. The appealing humility of his position appeared to be a well-devised substitute for lack of genius. Halfpence, occasionally pieces of bread, and even tobacco, came fast to his platter. He received alms in kind, as well as in coin, and those who had no money shared their next valuable commodity with him.

At the opposite ascent of the bridge was a second dark man. This rival levier of contributions was tall of stature and robust of frame. His face, even wanting the significance of the eyes, was such as you would place on the shoulders of your ideal man of eminence. His lips were decisively chiselled, and capable of the most varied inflexion; his nose was cast in the Roman mould, and his forehead was high, and expansive at the temples. His was a face that would arrest your attention and invite your study. Were he not a blind beggar, eminent as such, you would say that he should have taken the lead in some other more imposing position.

He was seated on one of the upright stones placed

along the bridge to prevent the inroad of vehicles to the footway. His glistening, jet-black locks—(he had as yet hardly seen his fortieth year)—escaped in profusion from the tasselled cotton nightcap covering his head. His staff was between his knees, and rested against his broad chest; in his left hand he held his hat for the reception of benefactions; with his right he gesticulated energetically,—ay, and even oratorically and gracefully. He turned on his stone seat as on a pivot, directing his words, now to the left, now to the right, now directly to the front. His sonorous and well-modulated voice was heard long before you reached him; and its cadences were so musical that it drew you to listen.

I have said that the eminent Irish beggar is a poetic beggar. And this dark man enounced his claims to the sympathy of the passengers as a genuine poetic Irish beggar can alone attain to, and in this wise:—

"Christian people, open your hearts of charity to the blind,—

"To the blind who cannot see the blessed light that shines for you.

" And from the heart of charity let the hand of charity be extended

" With relief, to the dark man afflicted by the Lord.

" The Lord has taken away the sight of my eyes, blessed be His name!

" And the Lord has said to the Christian man and woman—

" ' Relieve the blind man in darkness by My will.'

" Give your charity, Christian people, for the Lord's sake;—

" Give your charity, that it may be a store laid up in Heaven for you.

" Give your charity for the sake of your poor soul,

" That you carry with you, nursing it in its cradle of sin;

" Nursing it for a world to come.

" Where it will be born again—

" Born for sorrow,

" Or, born for glory!—

" Give your charity and earn the prayers of the blind of God!"

The humble dark man fared well the Christmas-eve I tell of. But the benefactions poured into the hat of this eloquent and poetic dark man at a marvellous rate.

The third dark man, and with him my business lies, stood above the centre arch of the bridge, his back resting against the balustrade. He was tall, six feet in height, if not taller,—his person in perfect symmetry and proportion with his stature. He might be fifty, or nearly so, but this it was not easy to determine. There were no wrinkles in his oval face, but although his whiskers were black, his hair was white. His head was thrown back somewhat; his sightless eyes were for the most part closed, yet occasionally the lids were raised from them. His finely-formed lips were hard-pressed together with an expression of deep, sombre sadness—sadness as if it were the gloom of a night that was to see no morrow.

His attire was of fine material, and well-fitting to his person. It was threadbare and much worn, but not ragged. It had been patched in many places, to conceal the rents made by time, and it was carefully brushed. Very remarkable, regarding him as a dark man craving charity, his linen, as seen at his breast and above his black silk handkerchief, was unsoiled and perfectly white. There is great significance of character — in the position of a hat on the wearer's head, and a fashion adopted in youth will, in most cases, be the fashion through life. In the instance of the dark man I am now noticing, his hat was placed somewhat to the left side of his head, and imparted to his air a tinge of levity in strong and strange contrast with the sorrow of his face.

This dark man was not eloquent, as was he of the pivot; nor was he lowly like him of the ill-fitting coat. He was altogether silent, his open left hand was stretched out from him, while with his right he leaned upon his staff.

Both of the other beggars had been frequently on the bridge before;—indeed the wearer of the ill-fitting coat was a fixture there. This silent dark man had never begged there until this Christmas-eve. Neither the eloquence of the eloquent beggar, nor the humility of the humble beggar drew as much attention or created as much commiseration as the silent appeal of the new-comer.

Both of the others had the advantage of position. They encountered the passers of the bridge at either end. Yet scarcely one went by without momentarily pausing to scan this taciturn dark man. Not one so pausing and examining that did not come to the conclusion that begging was a new occupation to him,—that he had seen better days,—that he had met with heavy calamity,—and that his heart had been crushed beneath the weight of his sorrows. Few of the observers who could command a humble offering passed by without laying it in his outstretched palm. And not one of the sympathizers who did not remark that the palm so extended was smooth, and had never been hardened by laborious occupation.

The offerings in the outstretched palm were abundant, and the simple "May God bless you!" of the recipient was received as ample return.

There was a singularity connected with this sad and silent beggar that drew as much, if not more, attention than the man himself. A blind man, and a blind man's dog, are close associations. Well skilled the blind man's dog ever is in his vocation. I never saw one so occupied that did not appear to understand his duty thoroughly, and to discharge it *con amore.*

The silent and sad dark man was not without his

canine companion, but the relation between them seemed to be reversed. "The car before the horse," it was shrewdly remarked to be. From appearances it was plain that in the present instance the blind man was the guide, not, as in all other cases, the follower, instructed by the sagacity of his dog.

In contact with the dark man's feet, as he stood patiently with outstretched hand, was a small four-wheeled cart, the string from which was passed round his wrist, and on a bed of fine and soft hay within this cart lay a dog. A large dog this was. To judge by the white muzzle resting on the edge of the rudely-fashioned machine, he was an aged dog—a very aged dog. His eyes, too, which in a dog of prime are so brilliant and expressive, gazed with lack-lustre vagueness at the objects moving within his contracted vision. Twice or thrice in the course of the day the animal crept, with much difficulty, out of his enclosure, staggered a little distance, returned, smelled to the blind man's legs, and lay down again within his cart.

On these occasions it was noted that the hair of the poor brute's coat was scant and staring; that he was attenuated and lank; that his head poked down helplessly; that his ears drooped heavily, and that his tail hung at full length, inert, and incapable of expressing sentiment or opinion. His bones seemed to be held together by the covering of the hide alone, while his limbs discharged their office in support or motion languidly and ineffectually. Yes—he was a very aged dog. A fine dog he must have been in his day, but now the termination of his existence from sheer age must be near at hand.

Was it not beyond precedent that this useless old dog should be so cared for in his infirmity? It certainly was a providence seldom if ever witnessed. That silent and sad dark man must have an affectionate heart. It was evident to those who compared notes on the matter that the dog had done his duty by him as long as his strength remained, and now the dark man cherished his faithful companion in his last days.

Neither the dark man on the pivot by his eloquence, nor the kneeling dark man by the lowliness of his humility, drew more sympathy from the passengers over the bridge than did the silent dark man by his gratitude and affection for his worn-out dog.

* * * *

As night closed in, the passengers over the bridge were few. Suddenly an energetic woman of middle age, clad in homely but comfortable guise, pounced on the kneeling dark man.

"We'll be going," she announced in a hasty whisper.

"That's Judy?"

"Yes, Darby. Stand up an' let us face home."

Judy assisted Darby to rise. The tails of the coat made to a measure for which he "was not at home" rested in the puddle when he stood to his full erectness. Judy shook the right skirt anxiously. It was very weighty, and in it a significant jingle.

"A great day, Darby, Lord be praised."

"Never a betther day this many years, Judy."

Darby placed his hand on Judy's shoulder, and away the dark man and his wife went in a trot, in gleeish but subdued colloquy.

* * * *

"Are you there?" the eloquent dark man on the pivot asked in a deep undertone.

"Here I am, sure enough."

He had a wife too;—she had for a short time been waiting near.

"What have you for supper?"

"Everything that's good."

"What is it?"

"Pig's cheek an' mealy potatoes."

"What else?"

"A quart of pale butt."

"Well?"

"Tay an' toast, if 'tis your fancy."

"Well?"

"A pint of the crathure—eh?"

"That'll do. Now step out like a greyhound. I'm starved wid the hunger—I'm perished wid the could. I'm dhry as unslaked lime, bawling and shouting here from day-dawn."

And off went the poetic dark man to his abundant supper.

* * * *

The silent man stooped down, and felt that his ancient dog was in his cart. He patted him with his hand, and feeling his way step by step, with his long piked staff, and drawing the dog's cart after him, he moved onward.

He descended the bridge, and entered the street of the town. He stopped occasionally to inquire his way, and it was a pleasing thing to see how he was conducted along.

Little children left their play, and took him by the hand, and led him on a while, then consigning him to other little children who stilled their shout, and received the dark man's hand reverently. And he was given in charge to old men, who led him carefully and gently onward. And young men agog for their evening's pastime took charge of him. And from the young men's care he passed into the charge of girls full of their maiden merriment, and his lowly "God bless you!" as he parted from each conductor was sufficient guerdon. In this wise the dark man, drawing his dog's cart, passed through the town and into the country, where the direct road was under his feet.

CHAPTER II.

PHIL MONAHAN, THE DARK MAN, AND HIS NEW FRIEND.

When a short distance from the town, the blind man and his ancient dog went on unguided, save that occasionally the dog's conductor inquired his way from any chance passenger. He had advanced about half a mile beyond the precincts of the town, and had reached the entrance gate, in the lodge of which I subsequently found Michael Hanrahan and Mary. Here he was interrupted in his progress.

A very inebriated man followed along the same road. He occasionally stood stock still, and entered into serious expostulation with himself regarding the sin of intemperance. It would appear, from the nature of the controversy carried on, that two beings were somehow resident within the same individual; one of these accusing the other of drunkenness, the other repelling the charge as a calumny advanced by a vile defamer, so drunk that "he could not see a hole in a forty-foot ladder," and who somehow mistook the perfectly sober Phil Monahan for himself. And Phil Monahan, having the best of the argument on his side in these frequent disputations, would express his sense of victory by a shout—which shout went far as evidence against himself. Simultaneous with the shout that rang far and near, Phil Monahan generally set forward at his tip-top speed. Occasionally he fell headlong,—no, not Phil Monahan, but the other fellow. And then there was a renewed contention between the sober and the drunken man; then another shout, and then another race.

Opposite the entrance gate he came up with the blind man.

"Hurroo!" he exclaimed, in tipsy indignation. "What is this for? Isn't that a dog I see there?—

Yes, I'm not purblind; the sighthe of my eyes tells me that it is a dog—a poor, honest dog, tied neck an' heels, an' a cursed peeler dragging him to the lock-up on the sthretcher. Maybe the dog took a few glasses—over much—an' no blame in the Christmas times. The peeler sha'n't put you in the lock-up, my dog. Get up!—get up an' come with your friend Phil Monahan! You shall not be taken to the lock-up,—if there was a score of peelers. Get up, poor dog—get up!"

To evidence his intention of being the dog's deliverer from thraldom, he kicked the object of his chivalry, and the enfeebled brute whined piteously.

The dark man suddenly turned, and seized the champion by the collar. Phil Monahan was no diminutive specimen of the human race,—a good-sized, short-built fellow, he was on the contrary,—but the dark man shook him as if he were a dwarf. For a moment he appeared irritated; but his anger passed away.

"Unhappy man, you are drunk!" he said, in a calm but impressive voice.

Indignantly and clamorously the slander was repelled. The blind man was a lying, false-swearing peeler; and Phil Monahan detested peelers, and was able to conquer a whole battalion of them!

Nor did he declare his hostility to peelers, and his purpose of onslaught, in mild accents. He roared out his threats in the furious manner in which outraged and slandered sober men will express their feelings.

The passers-by stopped to learn the cause of contention. Phil Monahan's voice rose to such a pitch, that persons at a distance heard him. Many ran fast to witness, as they hoped, a scrimmage, and twenty or more spectators were quickly assembled.

Phil Monahan used his fists, which were entirely at his disposal, at the same time that his lungs were strained to express his indignation. He struck the blind man two quick, following blows into the face. There was an instantaneous interference by the lookers-on. The sad, dark man who had begged on the bridge, and who had shown such affection for his worn-out dog, was recognized by nearly every one present. It was an outrage on all that was manly and Christian-like, to strike the dark man afflicted by the hand of God, and who could not see to defend himself.

Perhaps a flash of irritation may have passed across the blind man's face, when the two hard blows were given by Phil Monahan's clenched fists. But this too was momentary. He only pushed back his assailant, to the full length of his arm, and held him so. The succeeding blows fell short of their mark. He was called on by the general voice to loose his grasp of the bellowing drunkard; and he did so. And Phil Monahan was forced away by many hands, and he was dragged this way and that way; and he was hooted at for striking the dark man,—he insisting that he had been engaged in praiseworthy combat with a peeler. He gave work enough to all who could lay hands on him to hold him in durance; he had become frantic, and roared, and screeched, and bellowed at a furious rate. And nearly the whole of the assemblage talked together, so that there was an uproar.

The dark man held himself very erect.

"My friends," he said, "this poor man is lamentably inebriated;—do not injure him;—quiet him if you can. I have a duty to discharge towards you and him; I have a mission to fulfil. If I can obtain a hearing, my tale, the tale I have to tell you, may —the good God assisting—be a preservation to all that hear me."

He paused. The tumult of voices had drowned his words.

"It is useless at present," he sighed. "I cannot obtain a hearing."

As he spoke, the clamour receded from him. Phil Monahan had been mastered. Six men held his legs, and six men held his arms. And thus he was borne away, plunging to get loose, and shouting and "hoorooing" his defiance to the band of peelers holding him in bondage.

While the dark man stood and listened, a small, silky hand was placed within his. He turned his head, at the touch, and a gentle voice spoke up to him in a low but clear musical tinkle, as if a very little silver bell were struck with a tiny silver hammer.

"Come with me," the voice said, "away from this rude noise and contention."

"A lady speaks to me," the blind man returned, "a gentle and young lady, if I mistake not?—A very small and soft hand is this in mine;—voice and hand tell me I address a young lady."

"I am young, and I fill a lady's station."

"So I judged. Sweet-voiced and soft-handed young lady, I am blind, and a beggar for my daily sustenance. I am, you see, beneath your notice."

"That you are blind I know;—for that reason I have taken your hand to guide you. I ask it as a favour that you will be my guest to-night. Why do I make this request? Well—cannot you say that I am a spoiled child, indulged in all whims and fancies, and that I have set my heart on being your hostess for the night?—Will you not help to spoil me, as others do, and indulge me in my wish?"

"Young lady! if it be pastime at my—" the blind man hesitated, and did not finish the sentence he had begun. He resumed:—

"If amusement be your object in taking the blind beggar from his lowliness, there is little to be elicited from a man of many sorrows,—self-convicted as the author of his own misfortunes."

"Ah! do not—do not, pray, so misunderstand me! It is not in my nature, believe me, to trifle with you, or to pain you. I saw you to-day while you stood on the bridge, and I felt for you, not the mere commiseration that bestows a dole, but the true sympathy of the heart, for one who, I felt sure, had been reduced from worldly station to extreme indigence. You may rely on the sacredness of my word that I was going forth to seek you when I met you here. Do you not credit me?"

"It is singular,—very singular. But, young lady, I do believe you. There is no levity in the accents of your sweet voice, and I do trust you."

"Then you accept my invitation?"

"Young lady, I obey your wish."

"Then I shall be your guide. You may intrust yourself to my care."

Hand in hand, the blind man and his conductress went on together. They entered the gate at hand, and proceeded up the avenue.

CHAPTER III.

THE DARK MAN'S STORY.

The surmise of the blind man was correct;—his guide was young—not much beyond eighteen. He knew by touch and hearing, how velvety was her hand, how clear and musical her voice. He imagined her to be handsome; it were a pity, he thought, that the hand and voice should be matched with plain features. And the young lady *was* lovely, very lovely,—I can avouch this, as I had opportunity for judging at a shortly subsequent period.

Along a straight, old-fashioned avenue without twist or turn, they proceeded together. They crossed a bridge, the blind man knew, for he heard the water beneath chiming sweet water-music as he passed over. Up a gentle ascent they wended, and they reached the hall-door of the mansion house before glanced at.

"We are now at our destination," the silvery voice said. The door opened without a summons, and a young man who stood within the hall, came gently forward, in obedience to the lady's signal· and lifted the dog's cart inside. The blind man's escort smiled at this gentleman, as she and her captive entered, at the same time that she held up significantly her disengaged hand.

The young girl and her companion crossed the hall, and were entering a room at hand. The blind man hesitated when he had made a step or two beyond the threshold.

"If I mistake not, lady," he said, "I am entering a softly-carpeted apartment. Is not this unbefitting—as to myself—but more unseemly still that this humble friend of mine should accompany me? And from him I cannot part."

"Your dog shall accompany you and share your welcome—poor old fellow. Come along—you can no longer recede from me if you would. I have you in my power. You are in a fairy's palace, and I am the presiding fay. Here I am absolute, and to all who enter, the power of volition is of no avail. So come, and still place your faith in me."

While the young lady thus merrily spoke, she continued to draw the blind man onward. Her soft hands placed him in an easy chair, within the influence of a cheerful fire. She it was who drew the little cart towards him, so that when he put down his hand, it rested on the old dog's head, as he lay coiled up therein.

The blind man wondered and wondered at all this, and busied himself in the endeavour to surmise what was to be the upshot of his adventure. To the questions regarding his comforts, and to other passing queries, addressed to him while, as the blind man knew by her voice, and the rustling of her dress, his hostess moved about almost noiselessly, but briskly, he endeavoured to reply as best he might, but still he wondered exceedingly.

His fair entertainer rang a bell, and a servant

answered the summons. Directions were given in a low voice, and shortly a table was placed close to the visitor's arm-chair, and his circumscribed but acute senses told him that a repast was placed thereon; after which the servant retired.

The fairy of the enchanted palace ministered to him herself. Eagerly and hospitably she sought out his likings. She carved his meat for him with her own hands, and pressed him cordially, though not obtrusively, to partake of the fare she named to him for his selection. She filled out sparkling wine for him, but this he firmly though respectfully declined; he had pledged himself against the use of all fermented liquors, and to this pledge, he told her, he intended, with heaven's assistance, to adhere.

Then the blind man's attendant fairy knelt and fed the dog. Perhaps this act of tenderness touched him more than even her attention to himself.

"May God bless you, child," he said; while, as if unconsciously, he laid his hand upon her head, which touched his knee as she knelt. The head was not withdrawn while he gave his benediction.

A servant again answered the call of the bell. The table was removed, and again, as the blind man judged, he and his hostess were the only tenants of the room.

"Now," the lady said, drawing her chair close to that of her guest, "I have a favour to ask of you. You will not refuse me?"

"Lady, if it be within my power to comply with your wishes, it would ill become me to deny you."

"While I stood near you outside our gate, you said to the people there that you were desirous to tell them the tale of your misfortunes. May I—may I be your listener—instead of those unruly men?"

The blind man bent his head towards his chest, and remained for a few minutes in deep thought. When he raised it again, the lids were closed over his sightless eyes, but there was an unmistakeable expression of sadness and solemnity about his mouth. He spoke in a full, sonorous voice, deliberately, and as if his recollections awed him.

"Lady," he said, "in complying with your request, I but fulfil a mission, as I hope, nay almost believe,—deputed to me. The 'Ancient Mariner' of Coleridge, because he slew the albatross, was doomed to wander about and recite his tale wherever he could find a listener. Like to that 'Ancient Mariner,' I go from place to place, and I tell my story to whomsoever will hearken to me. The doom of the Ancient Mariner was driftless and unproductive, and his recital conveyed no moral save that slaying aught unnecessarily is to be avoided.

"Yet Coleridge's 'Ancient Mariner' gave me the first notion of my purpose, though in no respect, save that he recited his tale on all occasions, is there a parity between us. I shall not call my self-imposed duty a doom; it is a mission—for it is not, like the tale of the 'Ancient Mariner,' without object or advantage. The recital of my tale to all listeners has a two-fold aim. My main object is, to humble myself before men with sincere penitence of heart,—and in so doing, to humble myself before the God I have offended. May that God, in his mercy, and through the merits of His Son, accept my offering! My second purpose is, to give warning by my example, and thus induce others to shun the temporal and eternal misery which is the inevitable consequence of the crime of intemperance. As regards you, young lady, my tale is scarcely fitted for your ears. It is but the recital of a reckless continuation in sin, without a palliation for the criminality. Yet I fulfil the primary object of my self-imposed mission by avowing my sinfulness to one who pities the criminal because he suffers, without scanning the justice of his punishment. I but fulfil my mission by debasing myself before one who does not take into consideration that the fate of the drunkard is of his own contrivance. My kind young listener, I will, as a mark of my contrition, deprive myself of your sweet sympathy, by revealing the enormity of my offences."

The blind man had spoken fluently and energetically. He paused for an instant to collect his thoughts. Something was resting lightly on his knee. He placed his hand where he felt the gentle pressure; both the hands of his hostess were there clasped together, and were he not sightless he would have met the intent gaze of her soft, tear-suffused grey eyes. He gently pressed the clasped hands in his, in mute acknowledgment. Then he proceeded to his narrative.

"Some years ago," he said, "there was no young man throughout the length and breadth of the land with whom I would have changed places. I had in my possession all the elements of happiness; I had health, and energy, and power,—the energy to will, the power to execute. Confined to my legitimate sphere, I had abundance of worldly gifts, and the proud consciousness was mine that my abundance came to me from my own talent and industry, exercised in following an honourable and lucrative profession. For honourable *is* the profession I belonged to, if its duties be faithfully discharged.

"Nature had beneficently endowed me with a

joyous, elastic temperament that enabled me to spring up from the closest application light-spirited and cheerful, prompting me to good-fellowship with every one, and urging me to share my pleasurable sensations with all within my reach.

"Young lady, one essence only was wanted in my paradise. There is no pleasure in mere selfishness, no true gratification where enjoyment is not participated. Let philosophers preach up solitude as they may, youth and high spirits will not be solitary. The light of love was all I required to beam on me, and ripen my enjoyment into bliss.

"And love, pure, unalloyed, radiant love was given to me. I was beloved by a young heart, glowing with affection; and that heart was in the breast of one in outward form as lovely as the Creator's hand ever modelled.

"My wife, my beautiful Ellen, loved me with all her heart's fondness. And oh! I loved my Ellen with a passion that could not freeze—God knows I did! Believe me, child, that even in my uttermost abandonment—even while I was madly and profanely crushing my darling's tender heart to death, I loved my wife to adoration.

"In my self-accusation I have often thought that if a fiend were despatched from the place of eternal punishment, and that his mission was to seek out where human happiness had been bountifully disposed, and having found that abode of happiness to contaminate by his suggestions, and to blight and darken whatever he could not contaminate—I have said to myself that this fiend so commissioned would have entered under my roof. In what light then, am *I* to regard myself, who as effectually destroyed the happiness of my home as that fiend could have done?"

"Oh!" said the listener in a trembling voice, "your self-accusation is too harsh—too bitter."

"No, young lady, my self-accusals are merited. I became an incorrigible, irreclaimable drunkard. The fiend contaminated me, and then, as his agent, I perfected the work. I arraign myself before you, before the world, and before my God, as a murderer. Not actually as a shedder of blood—and yet a murderer. I was the cause indirectly of my children's death, and directly I was the destroyer of my wife, and more cruelly her destroyer than if with my hands I had taken her life. I was the slayer of my beautiful and beloved wife;—I slew her in return for her heart's devotedness.

"Oh God! Oh God!" the blind man exclaimed, and he turned up his sightless eyes, and smote his breast with his clenched hand.

"Oh God! Oh God!" he cried, "have mercy upon me!—have mercy upon me!"

The blind man's petition for mercy was a burst of passionate entreaty, and joining his hands together, he bent his head lowlily, and for a while prayed silently.

"Forgive me, young lady," he then resumed, in a moderated tone of voice. "Forgive me; I perceive that I have pained you."

The subdued emotion of his listener was not unnoticed by him. She was weeping, and the agitated breathing that heaved her bosom was detected by his ear.

"Unfortunately," he said, depressedly and sadly, "the tale I have to tell yields no pleasure to the hearer. It is a tale of sin, and of the woe that follows sin."

There was no answer; but the blind man's hand was pressed by the soft clasp that had led him to the easy chair in which he sat.

CHAPTER IV.

THE DARK MAN'S STORY ENDED.

The blind man bowed his head in thankfulness for the silent sympathy evinced towards him, and then resumed his story.

"When the second purpose of my mission is to be discharged;—when the reclamation of others, or their preservation from evil by the warning of example, are to be kept in view, I recount my step-by-step descent from comparative innocence to crime. Before you I present myself as a penitent; as a penitent I wish to appear before all who will so receive me. But I will not wound your ears by relating the gradation of my fall. It will suffice to tell you that I became a reckless, heedless drunkard, and that loss of station, loss of worldly substance, loss of home and happiness, and—were not God's mercy infinite—loss of the hope of salvation followed.

"Three of my lovely children died almost in their infancy; my wife took refuge from me in the grave.

"It will shock you to be told that as I followed the remains of my wife to the place of burial, I went with unsteady step, for I was intoxicated. The occurrences of that day come to me only as the reminiscence of a confused and horrid dream,—the recollection, as it were, of a phantom,—most appalling and terrific, grasping me with unconquerable power, but undefined and shapeless—vast and overwhelming.

"I remember that as I staggered behind my slaughtered Ellen's coffin to the graveyard, it appeared to me that I was the centre of a throng of accusing spirits that upbraided me as I went along. I remember looking down into the grave as the clay was tumbled in, and that I would have craved to be buried too, but that I knew I was unworthy to occupy the same resting-place with one so chaste and pure. I remember saying to myself that my dead wife would heave the coffin-lid and reject me, did I contaminate it by my touch.

"It is on my memory that I knelt at the grave's foot when it was covered in, and that I tried to pray, but that my tongue refused to utter, and that I durst not pray because of my unworthiness. I remember that I flung myself on the newly-tenanted grave in oblivious despair.

"I have now spent years probing my memory, to discover how long I may have so remained prostrate under the load of remorse that pressed on me with a mountain's weight. To this hour I cannot tell whether it was a night, or nights and days that I remained there. Nor can I inform you with anything like confidence in my accuracy as to the succession of events, whether it was while I supposed myself to be stretched on my wife's grave,—whether it was anteriorly, or whether it was subsequently,—that the astounding transfiguration I am now about to relate came to pass.

"Whether then, whether before, or whether after,

—this is certain. That bodily, I stood before the throne of God, to be judged by him,—to be judged for my iniquities;—to be judged for my riotousness and debauchery;—to be judged as the slayer of the children given to me for protection,—as the murderer of the wife of my bosom. I stood bodily before the throne of God for judgment."

"Oh no!—oh no!—the phantasy of a perturbed mind this was."

"Child, you are not the first to tell me so. Many have said the same. Therefore have I studiously subjected myself to close examination. Child! this was no phantasm. I have been enabled, through the cautious mental scrutiny of years, to separate the real from the illusive. I have been enabled to distinguish the abhorrent visions of grimacing imps, and the loathsome, crawling reptiles that my brain's delusion shaped, from the positive reality.

"I repeat it; I stood bodily before the throne of the Most High to abide my judgment. It was more an innate consciousness of the Presence in which I stood that told me this, than the evidence of my senses. There was a supernatural brightness all around me. I could discern the vibration of the celestial atmosphere, as the ethereal spirits passed me on their missions. But I could see naught beyond the great brightness; my unworthy eyes were not permitted to behold aught else. My ears were filled with Hallelujahs!—ever and ever floating through the air. I stood, as I knew and felt, in the Almighty Presence, shrinking and despairing. And when the "Gloria in Excelsis Deo" was chaunted by the Heavenly Choir I knew that my Judge was approaching, and I kept my lips hard-pressed against each other, lest blasphemies might issue thence,—blasphemies such as the fiends utter when their doom is for eternity!"

There was an insane working of the blind man's features as he went on with his description. The perspiration poured from his temples down his face, and both his hands were stretched forward to their utmost strain. He continued, speaking rapidly and energetically:

"A dazzling illumination appeared opposite to where I stood, and a voice, fearful in its intensity, issued thence. I heard the dread summons, 'Stand forward!'—and I moved towards the brightness. Even within the radiance, four forms rose slowly to my sight. My wife stood there in her grave-clothes, but radiated with the glory surrounding her. She looked on me with eyes of pity, yet I felt that she was there as my accuser before the throne. And my three children were there—angels I knew them to be, yet they glared at me in abhorrence. Then the voice, more astounding than the thunder-clap that rattles just above the head,—cried out, and pronounced my sentence.

"'Depart from me, you accursed,' it said. And at the same instant, another voice, like the hissing of a serpent formed to human speech, shrieked out—'*He is mine—he is mine—he is mine!*'—Oh!" the blind man broke in, dropping his hands, while his head suddenly drooped forward, and his voice sounded hollow and unnatural—

"Oh! the horror of that moment no words of

mine can tell! I sprang up and I raced forward. Whither to run I could not at first tell. I ran to escape from the fiend into whose custody I had been given. I ran—ran headlong.

"I remembered afterwards that I was hurled down precipices. That I buffeted the current of a river. That I scaled hills, and plunged into hollows. That I scrambled through thorny thickets. That I waded through deep morasses. But no obstacle could stay me. Step for step,—whether I tumbled, or whether I climbed, or whether I waded, or scrambled, or swam,—I heard the fiend almost in contact with me—in close pursuit. Wherever I went the fiend tracked me.

"I came within sight of the roaring sea, and I heard it thundering and chafing, hundreds of feet below me. I claimed kindred with the uproar of the mighty waters; I reached the highest cliff above the turmoil; I stooped my body, to give greater impetus to the death-plunge. On the extreme edge of the precipice, I was seized and held back, and pulled inward from the cliff. For a moment I struggled to get loose, that I might accomplish my deadly purpose. That moment of hesitation saved me. The dread of rushing unbidden into the presence of an angry God came upon me, and maniac that I was, I trembled. The superhuman vigour that had until now upheld me was no longer with me. At the same moment that the recollection of the eternal doom before me, if I presumptuously stood face to face with the Almighty, struck terror to my soul, the unnatural strength and resolution that had borne me up, faded away, and I fell forward, powerless and exhausted."

"It was the merciful Hand of God that stayed you!"

"Yes, young lady, in gratitude and thanksgiving I acknowledge the Divine interference. If, without even one tear of penitence, in the balance against my sins, I had audaciously forced myself into eternity, with the additional crime of self-murder on my soul,—I was lost, for time and eternity. Yes!—I do thankfully acknowledge the Hand of Heaven between me and the fate I had presumptuously dared to meet. God, in His Providence, often uses the simplest means to effect His wisest purposes. It was so in my case.

"There was an agency to which I owe my salvation. The agent was this dog that you see here near me now. This disabled dog that you see was my saviour. Even from my wife's grave he followed me; through all my wild race he followed me. While I couched, as does the tiger, preparatory to my spring from the cliff's brow, he it was—this my faithful dog!—that held me back. To him I owe it that time has been given me to weep over my offences. To him I owe it that the hope of mercy is mine.

"This feeble dog was then in his prime—robust and strong. And he held me from my doom, while the Divine mandate came forbidding my self-murder. My poor dog is now old and worn out; he has lived beyond the usual term of life given to his species. But as long as life is in him he shall share whatever the blind man has to share. For is he not my saviour—strong and faithful in his attachment, and the instrument of my preservation?"

"Indeed, indeed the noble brute deserves your attachment and your gratitude."

"I even owe to him more than I now tell you. I cannot tell how long I may have remained senseless where I fell. I was restored to consciousness by him. His tongue, gently licking my wounded face, was the first sensation I felt of my recovery. Then came the thought of quitting the spot where I had been tempted to self-slaughter. I was bruised and lacerated, and crept along with difficulty. The desire came on me to go away, no matter where; to the greatest possible distance from the scene of my transgression. The pride of nature was not yet subdued, and I loathed the idea of being seen or recognized. While it was yet dark I crept on. The first day I burrowed in a sandhill. The next night, I walked as fast as I could trail my wounded body. And when day came on again, I hid, as the beasts that roam by night hide themselves from the light. I was wounded from head to foot, and my progress was but slow. As I lay in my concealment, hunger, ravenous hunger gnawed me, and yet I would not go amongst my fellow-creatures to seek for succour. Would you believe it?—This dog, now so decrepit, brought me food, and we devoured it together. How he procured it I cannot tell, but more than once he fed me in my lair. On, on I went, though only through the darkness of night,—I knew or cared not whither. At length I sank, exhausted, and unable to proceed. My dog did not abandon me. I must have perished in the den of my concealment but for him. He sought aid, and charitable people came, and bore me to a refuge. In a workhouse far away from my native place I was placed. The story of my dog had gained friends for him, and he was not parted from me. I passed through a fearful probation of delirious disease. And for some months I lay, unable bodily or mentally to take care of myself. During the scramble from my wife's grave to the sea, my eyes had been lacerated, and I was told that thorns had been extracted from them.

When I went forth at length, I was blind. And now, for two years, I have begged for my sustenance where none could recognize me, or trace my disgraceful career."

For some time the blind man had spoken calmly and resignedly.

"And now," he said, sighing deeply, "my tale is told. I shall add but little more. I have told you that there is a self-imposed mission to be discharged. What this duty is, I have explained to you.

"My lowliness has brought with it a wholesome sense of humility. The pride which caused me to flee away from the scene of my prosperity and happiness has left me altogether. I am now travelling to the spot where my wife lies buried, that I may pray for forgiveness on her grave. I will no longer shun the scorn of those who knew me in the hey-day of my prosperity. I will humbly abide their recognition, and acknowledge the justice of their censure.

"Another object still, impels me to return whence I came. When I fled from the opprobrium of those who were cognizant of my transgressions, I had a son. He was a boy of splendid promise. In outward form and in feature, none could excel my boy. His, too, was a noble spirit. Daring, and brave, and generous he was, ardent and impulsive as a youth should be. But his manly nature was easily softened to gentleness when his affections influenced him. His mother's heart of devotion, and his mother's tenderness of nature, beautifully tempered his boyish impetuosity.

"Basely selfish as I was, I abandoned this glorious boy. Impelled by selfish pride, my only desire was to flee away without leaving a trace by which I could be tracked from the scene of my downfall. Mingled with my pride, there was self-detestation, and I found a surly gratification in subjecting myself to extreme hardships. I disguised my selfish pride by saying to myself: ''Twere better my boy should have no father than that he should be forced to hide his head and screen himself from identity with the degraded man whom all—even he—must abhor, as the slayer of his mother.'

"So I abandoned my boy. My flight from him

was the same as if I were dead to him, and the only bequest I left him was the evil of a tarnished name — which 'twere better he should repudiate. Twice opportunities offered to make cautious inquiries after my son, but I could gain no tidings of him.

"The pride that swayed me has, I hope, been replaced by penitence and humility. And I am now, as I have told you, on my way to kneel at my wife's grave. When there I will ask where I may turn to seek her son. From that grave I will follow in his track, and I will continue to wander, wherever the faintest footprint may guide me, until I find him. I will meet my son. But our meeting shall be in secret, there shall be no witness to it.

"I do not seek my boy from a worldly motive. I do not seek him to claim his recognition of the sightless beggar you have sheltered. Oh, no, no! Although my heart yearns to meet my deserted child, our meeting shall be, as I have said, without witness. I am resolved to travel far and near, to reach him. When I and my boy meet, I will kneel submissively to him. On my knees I will beseech of him, for the love of God, to grant me his forgiveness for the injuries I have heaped on his young head. On my knees I will implore him to grant me pardon in his own name, and then to pronounce a pardon in his mother's—in the name of that mother I so cruelly hustled into her early grave.

"In my very inmost heart I have cherished the hope that my supplication will not be unavailing. If I do not altogether misapprehend the character of my son, he will not refuse the boon his penitent father craves. Then, in return for the pardon granted, I will supplicate for heaven's blessing upon him. The blessing even of an unworthy father is of value to the child. Then I will depart from him—none but he and I knowing of the tie between us. Again I will wander away from him, begging for my subsistence as I now do. Never again will I obtrude myself on his presence. Nèver again shall he look on his unworthy father. I will not remain near him—a stumbling-block in his path.

"Father!!!"

Came from a manly, but agitated voice, close by the blind man's ear. While at the same time, the beggar's outstretched hand was eagerly grasped, and pressed with an ardent pressure.

"Father—dear, dear father!" echoed the weeping hostess. And as she so addressed him, she flung her arms round his neck, and her lips were pressed to his cheek.

The blind man rose from his seat, and stood to his full height. His forehead was raised upward, his brows were slightly drawn together, and his lips quivered.

"Who is it calls me father?" he asked in accents that told the depth of his emotion.

"Your son—the son you seek, father, holds your hand in his, while your daughter's arms are now round your neck. Your daughter she is, for she is your son's bride."

"Is it the voice of my deserted boy I hear acknowledging me as his father?"

"Richard O'Meara, your son, speaks to you, and

claims a child's right to succour and to love his father."

"Then you have been a listener to my tale—to the story of a penitent heart?"

"Father, I have been your sympathizing listener all through."

The blind man withdrew his hand from that of his son. Gently, but decisively, he unloosed the soft arms that clung to him. He knelt, and joined his hands together, and raised them upward to the full extent of his arms.

"God of mercy!" he prayed, "receive my thanksgiving for this thy goodness. Receive the thanksgiving of a grateful heart."

"My son—" he said, after a brief silence, "I wish to touch you with my hands, for I am blind, you know, and cannot see you."

"I am close to you, father."

The blind man stretched out both his hands, and grasped his son's knees.

"You have heard my tale," he cried out, "and you know why it is that I was wandering in search of you. Here, kneeling at your feet, I supplicate your forgiveness. My son, I am a humble petitioner for your pardon,—pardon for the heartless injustice I have done you,—pardon for your father's criminal example to your boyhood."

"Father, father!" expostulated the young man, "do not humiliate yourself thus. It is unnatural. Rise, father, rise!"

And he endeavoured, but in vain, to raise the kneeling suppliant.

"From this contrite position I will not rise, my son, until I feel your hand upon my head, and hear your voice pronounce my pardon. Pardon—pardon for my sins against yourself!—and, oh! pardon for ny still more heinous offences against your mother!"

"Father," the young man answered, laying his hand upon his parent's head, and speaking in a voice so broken that it was scarce articulate, "father! from my heart do I forgive you. In my own name, and in my mother's name, I forgive you. Rise, father,—rise."

The blind man snatched the hand that rested on

his head. He pressed his lips against it fervently. As he did so, the tears gushed from his sightless eyes, and fell fast upon his pledge of pardon. And when he arose, still weeping, he turned his face upward, and prayed.

While the union between father and son progressed, the ancient dog, Teague, raised himself in his cart. By his scent he understood that his playmate of former days held intercourse with his master. He attempted to enunciate his old-times Wow—wow—wow of recognition. But the feeble whine of age mingled with its bygone mellowness.

The dog Teague was not the only approving party to the union of parent and child. When young Richard O'Meara first advanced from the obscurity of the room to accost his father, another figure moved forward at the same time. This other person progressed in a somewhat irregular manner. He carried a stout cudgel, which he raised up and put down as noiselessly as possible, so as to produce no sound by contact with the carpet. Leaning on his stealthy cudgel, he put his left foot forward very softly, a step in advance; then he crimped himself to one side, that he might draw off the second support of his body. This he raised with all imaginable caution, and placed it carefully beneath him. So he made his way, as silently as a cat could creep. Close by the blind man's chair he stood undetected, as erect as a statue; and when the son had pronounced his father's forgiveness, and while they stood hand-in-hand together, the Half-pay saluted the blind man's shoulders with a thwack of his cudgel, while he barked out—

"Maw—maw!—Wel-come!—Wel-come!"

Teague emitted for the second time his Wow—wow—wow of recognition, in the whine of tottering senility. For he recollected the Half-pay's voice, and his faculties being blunted by extreme old age, he supposed that his fast friend the Half-pay had addressed him personally, by inviting him to shake hands, as in the days of yore.

CHAPTER V.

CONCLUSION.

My narrative and its sequel have now been brought to a close. What I have further to say I will tell as briefly as I can. I do not myself like to be held by the button listening to tiresome recapitulations, and I will not detain the reader's button between my finger and thumb longer than need be.

In the Manor House where the union between father and son was accomplished, the person hitherto known as the Half-pay was born. In childhood he was a mischievous urchin. Whatever commands might be issued were no laws to him; no corner of the house was free from his intrusion; and wherever he penetrated, mischief done left traces of his visit.

In his boyhood he preferred any pastime to the restraint of sitting in a schoolroom, gaping stupidly at a book; and neither the cat-o'-nine-tails, then in vogue, or the horsewhip at home had any effect in communicating a taste for letters. On one occasion his stern, uncompromising father had had him tied to a staple in a dark room, where he was to be left in durance until his outlaw spirit should be subdued. He set to work with his teeth, however, severed the rope that held him in bondage, and, immediately following his restoration to liberty, he might be seen mounted bare-backed on the best hunter in his father's stable, and close up with the hounds full cry in pursuit of a fox. And home he rode triumphant, rope and staple entirely forgotten, with Reynard's brush in his cap, accorded to him by the acclamation of the field.

There were two persons in the Manor House who could control him—his mother, and a sister one year younger than himself. Scamp as he was, his mother loved him; for he would press her in his arms until she cried for quarter. To his mother's gentle remonstrance he always yielded for the immediate time. And in his sister's case, the fable of the wolf and the lamb was reversed. The wolf trotted in the footsteps of the lamb, whenever the lamb caressed the wolf.

His mother died. One governing impulse was gone, and the lamb's persuasion was only occasional. When his father and his steady, well-conducted cunning and condemning brother spoke of him, they called him the "rebel,"—and a rebel to authority he certainly was.

When his manhood came on he acknowledged no constraint. Unless the horses were put away, he rode them when he fancied, one after the other, without regard to ownership. He scattered the coveys of partridges the nineteenth of September, without waiting for the legal day. He danced at patterns, romped with girls wherever he met them, and—he was very often tipsy.

In his twentieth year, while his exemplary brother was in council with his father, increasing the rent-roll and controlling the expenditure, he, "the rebel," fell in love with the daughter of a neighbouring gentleman farmer, in station beneath himself.

For him the "light of love" was a furnace-fire, self-consuming, if no soluble material were supplied. The object of his attachment was very beautiful—her beauty had set the furnace blazing. She was very gentle, and her admirer's ardent addresses rather terrified her, and made her shrink from all contact. She refused to be consumed, and her white-heated lover determined on abduction. He succeeded in carrying her off, but she was rescued from him. He was compelled to fly to avoid the consequences of his illegal act, and his inflamer married her deliverer, to whom she had been long engaged.

When a year or two had passed by, his sister heard from him. He had enlisted as a soldier, and was then in a regiment of the line as a non-commissioned officer. Family pride induced his father to purchase an ensigncy for him, and at Corunna, where Moore was interred "with his martial cloak around him," my hero, then holding the rank of captain, received two dangerous wounds. A ball took advantage, while he was shouting to his men, to enter his open mouth, and passing through his neck, injured his colloquial organs. Hence his few words. His leg was also shattered above the knee; amputation was pronounced necessary. Hence the necessity for a wooden leg, transformed subsequently, as has been narrated, into a composite leg.

Quitting the wars, when needs must, he made his way home to the place of his birth. His father was dead. His sister having made an imprudent love-match, had been left a widow with one daughter to maintain on scanty means. His brother, now lord paramount, was a grasping, dishonest miser. The captain was tipsy when he presented himself to his nearest relative; this nearest relative disowned him. And so, with fifty pounds per annum, in addition to his half-pay—a long arrear being due to him,—he shook the dust from his feet at the paternal threshold, and set off, he knew not or cared not whither. He was set down, as we have seen, in "The Town of the Cascades."

The Half-pay's reverence for Ellen O'Meara was not of instantaneous growth. She was the daughter of his first and only love, and as like her mother as she could be in features and character.

The Half-pay's brother was the dishonest guardian who retained the orphan's dower until obliged by legal process to disgorge it.

From this it will be understood why, exclusive of personal attachment to the boy, the Half-pay adopted the grandson of the terrified girl who had made a soldier of him.

A few days previous to the death of Ellen O'Meara the Half-pay had received an intimation from his agent—the letter still addressed to the mysterious P. W.—that his brother had died childless and intestate, and that he was the legal inheritor of a large property.

Shortly after arriving at his mansion with his knapsack on his back and his adopted son by the hand, he learned that his sister had died, leaving her daughter very poor. He brought the little girl to his home, and, in his own way, was a kind father to her. His adopted son and his niece, just as he wished it to be, became fondly attached to each other, so without loss of time he joined their hands at the altar.

The Christmas-eve with which the sequel of my narrative opens, the Half-pay, now Captain Patrick Wemyss of Wemyss Hall, stumped through the town near at hand, accompanied by his niece. He remarked the silent beggar on the bridge. He was almost certain of his man, but under the long-settled belief that Richard O'Meara had perished in the sea, he resolved to make himself quite certain regarding him.

He communicated his suspicions to his niece, without consulting his adopted son; and at his suggestion, urged by her own goodness of heart, she was setting out to ascertain the reality of her uncle's surmises, when she met the blind man on the road.

The blind Richard O'Meara was not long domiciled with his son, until Michael and Mary Hanrahan were sought out, and raised to what they regarded as great opulence. Mary was the young wife's friend and adviser; Michael was the factotum of the household. Captain Patrick Wemyss of Wemyss Hall, was the blind man's guide and assistant whenever he went forth to fulfil his mission. Teague, the ancient mastiff, died of extreme old age shortly after his renewed intimacy with Captain Patrick Wemyss, the Half-pay.

And so ends the sequel to my narrative.

THE END.

CPSIA information can be obtained
at www.ICGtesting.com
Printed in the USA
LVHW040023180422
716440LV00005B/458

9 783752 595321